LET'S GET KRAKEN

Author:
Ken Spencer

Editors:
Jeff Harkness

Swords & Wizardry Conversion:
Jeff Harkness

Art Director:
Casey Christofferson

Layout:
Suzy Moseby

Interior Art:
Santa Norvaisaite, Adrian Landeros

Cartography:
Robert Altbauer

Front Cover Art:
Adrian Landeros

Cover Design:
Casey Christofferson

Necromancer Games
ISBN: 978-1-6656-0176-4
SW PoD

TABLE OF CONTENTS

LET'S GET KRAKEN

By Ken Spencer

A Swords & Wizardry adventure for 2–6 characters of levels 5–7

Let's Get Kraken is an adventure for 2–6 characters of levels 5–7. A good mix of characters is needed. The adventure puts the characters up against a kraken, a creature of legendary scale that they likely have no hopes of facing in open battle. Yet there is hope, for the kraken is under the control of a mad sorcerer bent on revenge. Stopping the sorcerer should stop the kraken, but there are other ways to save the town of Ostin and its fishing fleet.

In addition to the main plot, the adventure offers up the Wievin Strip, a stretch of coastline along the southern edge of Kadalon Bay. Once the town of Ostin is saved and the characters are hailed as local heroes, they can use Ostin as a launching point to explore the rest of the Wievin Strip or for further adventures in the Sundered Kingdoms.

Dramatis Personae

The following non-player characters appear in this adventure

Name	Description	Main Description
Sana Bel'vir	female human noble	Part Three: The Wievin Strip
Jisa Bel'vir	female human commoner	Part Three: The Wievin Strip
Katti and Matti Bartlett	female human commoners	Part Two: Trouble in Ostin
Arvsk Blackaxe	male dwarf bandit leader	Part One: Adventure Overview
Priest-Sergeant Kas Fellblow	male human priest	Part Three: The Wievin Strip
Wave Mistress Harfi	female human priest	Part Two: Trouble in Ostin
Eso Hightower	male human cultist	Part Two: Trouble in Ostin
Mayor Horsby	male human noble	Part Two: Trouble in Ostin
Baroness Lizatha Husbridge	female human noble	Part Three: The Wievin Strip
Wave Tender Kros	male human priest	Part Two: Trouble in Ostin
Jasitlia	female human bandit	Part Two: Trouble in Ostin
Captain Sahn'du	male human pirate captain	Part One: Adventure Overview

PART ONE: ADVENTURE OVERVIEW

The fishing town of Ostin on the shores of Kadalon Bay is famous for its annual grulin run, a time of year when the succulent and tasty fish spawn in the waters offshore. Although the town harvests other fish and sea life year-round, the annual grulin run boosts the town's economy and allows Ostin's residents to enjoy a measure of wealth above that of other fisherfolk. The time for the run is approaching, but the fishing boats are pulled up on shore, and no sane man or woman will venture out to sea.

Recently, a large creature with mighty tentacles attacked several boats, drowned their crews, and dragged the vessels beneath the waves. Ostin's mayor is very worried, as the fishermen may miss the grulin run and also be unable to bring in their regular catches. He entreats the characters to help him and his town defeat the beast that threatens to pauperize the fishermen and the townspeople who depend on them for their livelihood.

The kraken is only a small part of the problem, and one that the heroes may well be unable to face. The true threat is in the form of a sorcerer with a grudge against the town. Kaltran Bel'vir was born in Ostin, and two years ago his parents were tried and executed on false charges of consorting with demons. Kaltran swore vengeance. After spending a year and a half searching ancient ruins and moldering libraries, he uncovered a ritual that allowed him to summon the kraken.

Kaltran's Tale

Never a popular person in Ostin, Kaltran was a sullen and private youth who grew into a tall and dour adult. His parents were some of the village's most prosperous fisherfolk, owning their own boat and shares in the boats of other fisherfolk. It is the latter that truly made their wealth as they collected a percentage of every catch. This didn't win them any friends in town, especially as they were heavy-handed collecting what was due to them. This added to the social ostracism Kaltran suffered, but it also allowed the Bel'virs to hire the best tutors for their only child, as well as to import expensive books from distant cities.

Signs of Kaltran's sorcerous powers showed just as he entered manhood, further distancing him from his neighbors. Bitter toward all, he finally fled the town to seek power and knowledge in strange lands, vowing never to return. The town breathed a sigh of relief to see such a surly youth with mystical powers leave, but his parents were devastated by the loss. They turned their sorrow toward their business and increased their hold on Ostin's fishing fleet.

For five years, the young sorcerer wandered wide and far, and even fought trolls in the Northlands and orcs in the Northmarches. Rumors filtered back to Ostin that Kaltran had made pacts with foul beings, and that he was even involved in the Xanges River Massacre. However, the townsfolk of Ostin tended to focus on the darker rumors rather than on any heroic deeds accomplished by the scion of the Bel'vir family.

Eighteen months ago, a wandering witch hunter named Jarlitha the Pious came to Ostin. She sought to root out any heresy in town and soon ingratiated herself to the mayor and the leading citizens. With the full approval of Baroness Husbridge, Jarlitha began a series of inquests, but it soon became obvious that a heretic or three would be found no matter what was actually uncovered. Soon, the witch hunter's goons held a firm hold on the town, and the fearful citizens began offering up evidence, or at least testimony, that increasingly pointed to Kel and Olia Bel'vir being witches, heretics, and in league with dark powers. In the end, under torture, the Bel'virs confessed to being heretics in league with Kunulo the Hungering Tide. The trial was swift, and the couple were burned in the town square on a warm, sunny afternoon. Their vast wealth was divided among the witch hunter, the baroness, and the mayor, who to his credit distributed his share among those long under the thumb of the Bel'virs' economic might.

Kaltran's Revenge

Kaltran Bel'vir soon learned of his parents' execution, and he vowed to return to Ostin and reduce the village to ruins. Toward that end, he spent much of his money and several months researching his revenge. Although he was by then a powerful sorcerer well-versed in arcane mysteries, Kaltran was far too theatrical to simply march on Ostin and burn it to the ground. To further his plans, he sought the *horn of the kraken*, a magical artifact given by the sea god Quell to his high priest during the height of the Hyperborean Empire. The artifact was lost during the fall of the empire and the ensuing twilight of civilization, but Kaltran eventually discovered its location: the Temple of Tides north of Ostin.

Unfortunately, the magic-user found the temple abandoned, its treasures looted, and its priesthood scattered. Baroness Husbridge — at the urging of Priest-Sergeant Fellblow of the Church of Mithras — closed all temples, shrines, and other places of worship that did not honor the noble god of warriors. Such temples, Fellblow claimed, led only to greater strife and the possibility of heresy, as evidenced by the Bel'virs, who were regular patrons of the god Quell. No doubt, this association with Quell's temple led them to worship Kunulo, the sea deity's demonic shadow. However, the temple's greatest treasure was missed when the temple was ransacked, and the *horn of the kraken* remained hidden beneath the unconsecrated altar.

Kaltran claimed the horn and relocated to Tern Island in Kadalon Bay.

The isolated rocky island was home to a Hyperborean fortress that had long ago fallen into ruins. Kaltran cleansed the fortress of the creatures inhabiting it, then set about enacting the ritual to use the magic horn.

He finally succeeded, and two months later, the kraken attacked Ostin's fishing fleet.

Involving the Characters

You can involve the characters in the adventure in several ways. The easiest is for them to hear about the kraken attacks occurring in Kadalon Bay. Such events are the stuff of which heroes are made. They might also hear that the mayor of Ostin is offering a rich reward for anyone who slays the kraken. Stories vary, but the reward is said to be as high as 20,000 gp plus lodging at the Salmon and Shark. Finally, a character might have family in Ostin and hear from them about the troubles the town is facing.

Once the characters are in Ostin, help them establish a connection with the people of the town. Play up the townsfolks' friendliness and welcoming nature by using NPCs most likely to endear themselves to the characters. That way, when things turn bad, the characters have something more to fight for than just pay. Thus, heroes are born.

Stopping the Kraken

Adventurers being the resourceful types that they usually are, the characters are likely to come up with their own plans on how to stop the kraken's attacks. Use the following possibilities to better gauge the effectiveness of the characters' plans or to give them hints if they get stuck.

Kill Kaltran

By far the most obvious but not easiest solution is simply to find and kill Kaltran Bel'vir. The clues should lead the characters to Tern Island as they investigate the source of the kraken's attacks. Assaulting the fortress is difficult, but sneaking in and killing Kaltran is an option. He is a powerful foe, but his death ends the threat of the kraken. However, if he dies while the kraken is loose in the world, the beast is free to go about its business, which likely includes attacking the fishing boats.

Kill the Kraken

Ha, ha, ha. No really, stranger things have happened. The kraken is a mortal creature, and a very cunning, lucky, or overpowered party of adventurers might be able to kill it. Once dead, it can't be summoned again, so there is that. Kaltran might still be around and looking for revenge, however, and now he has a target: the adventurers who killed his kraken.

Reverse the Ritual

This might be even trickier than killing the kraken. The characters could steal the secrets of the ritual and the required items from Kaltran and reverse it. Maybe they do this after they kill Kaltran. This follows the same rules for awakening the Island that Dreams, though it requires targeting the kraken and the special ritual items used to summon the sea monster.

Awaken the Island that Dreams

While it is more expensive and time consuming than simply killing Kaltran and far easier than killing the kraken, the Island that Dreams can be awakened and used against the kraken or Kaltran. The island is a huge dragon turtle and can thus travel on land. Getting the components is rather simple, but finding the last one might be trouble if the characters don't spend time talking to the locals.

Kaiju Fight!

If the characters use the Island that Dreams to fight the kraken, there is the problem of the protagonists of the story sitting by while two monsters fight it out. That would be a shame. Instead, let the players take turns controlling the dragon turtle or one of its minions during each round of combat. When the Island that Dreams awakens, a giant shark for each player not directing the actions of the dragon turtle arrives from the depths to join the fray! Any **giant shark** that is slain is replaced by a **killer whale**, and then a **large shark**. After that, the heroes are on their own. The sea god can provide only so much help.

Killer Whale: HD 12; **AC** 4[15], **Atk** bite (3d10); **Move** 0 (swim 24); **Save** 3; **AL** N; **CL/XP** 12/2000; **Special:** none. (*Monstrosities* 508)**Large Shark:** HD 8; **AC** 6[13]; **Atk** bite (1d8+4); **Move** 0 (swim 24); **Save** 8; **AL** N; **CL/XP** 8/800; **Special:** feeding frenzy (1-in-6 chance of attacking another shark). (*Monstrosities* 420)

Giant Shark: HD 13; **AC** 5[14]; **Atk** bite (1d10+8); **Move** 0 (swim 18); **Save** 3; **AL** N; **CL/XP** 13/2300; **Special:** feeding frenzy (1-in-6 chance of attacking another shark). (*Monstrosities* 420)

Kraken Attacks and Other Events

The **kraken** attacks every other day, taking a ship or more down to the depths and eating the crew. Keep this pace up; it puts pressure on the characters to resolve the situation, and the longer it takes to stop the kraken, the more frustrated the townsfolk become. This might very well result in the characters being run out of town, but true heroes won't let that stop them from saving the day.

In addition to the horrifying attacks,

the following events occur during the adventure but are only tangentially related to the main plot. They provide situations that the characters must deal with immediately or that may be used to spur further adventures once they deal with the kraken.

Kraken: HD 20; **HP** 145; **AC** 0[19]; **Atk** 6 tentacles (2d6 + constrict), bite (3d6); **Move** 0 (swim 3, jet 21); **Save** 3; **AL** C; **CL/XP** 24/5600; **Special:** constrict (automatic 2d6 damage after hit, Open Doors check –1 [minimum 1] to escape), control weather (as spell), create lights (similar to will-o'-the-wisps, no attack), ink cloud (80ft-by-80ft-by-120ft cloud, 1d4 damage for 4 rounds if in cloud, save avoids). (*Monstrosities* 281)

The Baroness Arrives

Baroness Lizatha Husbridge arrives in Ostin around midday with her entire entourage (**5 knights**, **10 guards**, **15 commoners**, and **Priest-Sergeant Fellblow**). The baroness has heard of the trouble in Ostin and has come to perform her feudal duty. She and the priest-sergeant are arrogant, condescending, and demanding toward the townsfolk. For the most part, they do not speak directly to anyone of lowly station, though if one of the characters is a noble, they are shown due respect (spoken to directly, invited to dine with the baroness and Fellblow, treated with some decency).

Baroness Lizatha Husbridge, Female Human Noble: HP 12; **AC** 9[10]; **Atk** none; **Move** 12; **Save** 14; **AL** N; **CL/XP** 3/60; **Special:** none. (*Monstrosities* 254)

Kas Fellblow, Confessor Priest of Mithras (Clr7): HP 35; **AC** 3[16]; **Atk** *+1 flail* (1d6+1); **Move** 12 (swim 18); **Save** 9; **AL** N; **CL/XP** 7/600; **Special:** +2 save versus paralyzation and poison, banish undead, spells (2/2/2/1/1).

Spells: 1st—*cause light wounds* (x2); 2nd—*hold person*.
   Equipment: *gauntlets of swimming and climbing,* plate mail, *+1 flail, ring of poison resistance,* holy symbol of Mithras.

Commoners, Male or Female Humans (15): HD 4 hp each; **AC** 9[10]; **Atk** weapon (1d6); **Move** 12; **Save** 18; **AL** L or N; **CL/XP** B/10; **Special:** none. (*Monstrosities* 254)

Guards, Male or Female Humans (10): HD 1; **HP** 6 each; **AC** 7[12]; **Atk** short sword (1d6); **Move** 12; **Save** 17; **AL** N; **CL/XP** 1/15; **Special:** none. (*Monstrosities* 257)

Knights, Male or Female Humans (5): HD 3; **HP** 18 each; **AC** 5[14]; **Atk** longsword (1d8); **Move** 12; **Save** 14; **AL** N; **CL/XP** 3/60; **Special:** none. (*Monstrosities* 256)

The baroness arrives with great fanfare and immediately summons the mayor. She demands rooms for herself and her entourage at the Salmon and Shark, which means forcing out anyone currently staying there (including the characters). She then chews out Mayor Horsby about the situation in town. The baroness's words can be heard up and down the street. She belittles the mayor, explaining that hiring adventurers is a slight toward her and her noble family, and orders that they be dismissed. Chastised, Mayor Horsby flees to tell the characters the bad news, but begs them to stay on as his guests at the Hooked Hand until he can set the situation right.

The baroness and Priest-Sergeant Fellblow remain closeted at the inn for the rest of the day, but during this time, her entourage is busy about town. The guards maintain a five-person watch over the baroness, but those who are off duty can be found in the Hooked Hand drinking and causing trouble. The commoners attend to their mistress, but a few run errands while others meet with friends and family in the town. Despite how harsh the baroness can be as an employer, no one in her entourage is willing to speak ill of her. However, clever roleplaying, bribes, and buying rounds of drinks at the Hooked Hand might yield some of the following:

The baroness is in Ostin to slay the kraken and demonstrate her fulfillment of her noble rights.

Two years ago, the only child of the baroness ran away to become an adventurer. He died a few months ago, and his body was brought home for burial.

The baroness profited greatly from the Bel'virs' execution, taking the lion's share of their property and declaring their absent son a heretic *in absentia*.

Priest-Sergeant Fellblow has served as the baroness's confessor for many years, listening to her words and offering spiritual counsel. He is a fervent follower of Mithras and encourages the baroness to suppress all other gods within her domain. His influence led to the closing of the temple of Quell.

The baroness plans to harpoon the kraken so her guards and the fisherfolk can drag it ashore. She is commandeering *Ostin's Pride*, the largest fishing boat in town, for the task, as well as the smaller *Hort and Daughters* to carry her and Fellblow out to observe the action. A flotilla of smaller vessels join the hunt.

Unfortunately, the hunt does not go well. Kaltran's spy — a man named Eso Hightower (see Tower House [**Area O-14**]) — alerts him to the plan, and the kraken is waiting. Unless the characters intervene, the hunt is a disaster. The baroness and Fellblow are pulled beneath the waves, and all the ships involved sink with great loss of life. In the aftermath, the mayor apologizes and offers the characters their rooms back in the Salmon and Shark. If they so desire, the characters can renegotiate for higher pay.

The Storm

Clouds moving in from the north portend a massive storm brewing out to sea. In a matter of hours, the day changes as winds whip the sea to foam-capped peaks. The town is protected by the headlands of the Hook, but not entirely. Houses along the Hook are flattened, and a strong crosscurrent forms just offshore. Travel at sea is impossible and continues to be so for 1d6 days. Torrential rain floods the lower parts of the town and any depression in the lands beyond. The Bay Road becomes an impassable strip of mud where it is not covered by the rising tides.

This is a great time for the characters to interact with anyone in town with whom they have not yet had the time to speak. In addition to finding clues, they can help evacuate the cottages on the Hook, save people from collapsed buildings, and even take part in a few dramatic rescues from the flooded parts of town. The new temple (**Area O-12**) is one of the buildings that collapses during the storm. Although no one is inside, many see it as an omen. Any actions taken to help the townsfolk endear them to the people of Ostin and make any attempts to gain information much easier. Finally, due to the weather, Kaltran's spy is unable to communicate with him, thus giving the characters an opportunity to take out the spy without Kaltran becoming aware of the loss for a few days.

Strange Visitors

The day after the storm, the cog *Wave Dancer* limps into Ostin. Her main mast is gone and her crew suffered several losses from the storm. The ship is captained by Sahn'du (male half-orc **bandit captain**) and is carrying a cargo of wool to Highreach. The ship takes a few days to repair, but the captain is desperately short of crew and offers top coin (7 sp a week and a quarter share of the profits). This entices many of the younger fisherfolk; in the end, 12 are chosen to go (nearly a quarter of the town's population of young fisherfolk). This causes some hostility between the townsfolk and the visitors.

The *Wave Dancer* is not what she seems. While she does have a hold full of wool, the bales were not purchased at Endhome as her captain claims. They were in fact taken off the *Sunset Runner* after Captain Sahn'du and his pirates took the ship (and then burned it to the waterline to cover their tracks). A closer inspection of the ship is possible if someone gets aboard, but the captain and the remaining **3 crewmembers** are not letting anyone on the ship. Characters who do investigate the ship find evidence that it is more than it seems, with an increased number of crew accommodations, weapons stored in ready lockers, far too many weapons for a small merchant ship, wooden shields at the ready to cover the forecastle and stern castle, and bloodstains on the deck.

The ship can be hired to carry the characters to Tern Island at the price of 1,000 gp, with at least half up front. This might be steep, but it is likely far safer than taking a fishing boat that draws the kraken's attention. Sahn'du happily drops the characters off and pledges to remain just off shore to await their return. In truth, as soon as the characters are out of sight, the *Wave Dancer* hoists sail and is on her merry way.

Sahn'du, Male Human Pirate Captain (Ftr8): HP 59; AC 3[16]; **Atk** *+2 longsword* (1d8+4); **Move** 12 (swim 18); **Save** 5 (+2, ring); **AL** C; **CL/XP** 8/800; **Special:** −1[+1] dexterity AC bonus, +1 to hit missile bonus, +2 to hit and damage strength bonus, multiple attacks (8) vs. creatures with 1 or fewer HD.

Equipment: *+1 leather armor, +2 longsword, ring of protection +2, gauntlets of swimming and climbing,* leather sack containing 5d6 gp, 2d8 sp, and a diamond ring (250 gp).

Pirates, Male or Female Humans (3): HD 3; **HP** 18 each; **AC** 5[14]; **Atk** short sword (1d6) or belaying pin (1d4); **Move** 12; **Save** 14; **AL** C; **CL/XP** 3/60; **Special:** none. (*Monstrosities* 256)

Equipment: short sword, belaying pin (club), 1d4 sp.

Bandit Attacks

A rider in the middle of the night raises an alarm and claims bandits attacked several outlying farmsteads and are now moving toward Ostin. With the baroness and most of her guard dead (assuming she carried out her plans to find the kraken), Ostin is largely undefended. The town guard consists of only six members. Since there is no wall or other fixed defenses, the townsfolk talk of fleeing, but to where?

A known bandit leads a group of young thugs on the Bay Road, but the rider insists that these raiders are part of a different group. The people of Ostin still assume the bandits are just those on the road, however, and spread rumors to that effect.

The new bandits are actually a large force Kaltran hired as a distraction while he brings the kraken into the harbor to destroy the fishing fleet. The bandits arrive 16 hours after the warning goes up, marching down from the north in two columns. **Arvsk Blackaxe**, an infamous dwarf bandit, leads **30 bandits**. They were paid to attack the town, not take it, and to do their best to sow all manner of chaos. They attack for 10 rounds and then melt into the hinterlands before reforming and returning in a few days. While fighting, they start fires and loot.

Arvsk Blackaxe, Male Dwarf Bandit Leader (Ftr6): HP 41; **AC** 4[15]; **Atk** *+2 war hammer* (1d4+4); **Move** 9; **Save** 9; **AL** C; **CL/XP** 6/400; **Special:** +1 to hit and damage strength bonus, +4 save vs. magic, darkvision (60ft), detect stonework, multiple attacks (6) vs. creatures with 1 or fewer HD.

Equipment: *+1 chainmail, +2 war hammer,* small figurine of a whale (50 gp), 2d6 gp.

Bandits (30): HD 1; **HP** 4 each; **AC** 7[12]; **Atk** short sword (1d6); **Move** 12; **Save** 17; **AL** C; **CL/XP** 1/15; **Special:** none. (*Monstrosities* 254)

Equipment: short sword, 1d4 sp.

If Kaltran's spy is still in Ostin, he notifies his master when the bandits attack so the kraken can be summoned. The kraken arrives on round four of the bandits' attack and begins wrecking the ships in the harbor. By the time the bandits leave, the kraken has moved on to attacking any ships pulled up onshore. It takes the kraken 15 rounds to destroy all the ships in Ostin's fleet. It flees if reduced to below 75 hit points.

The destruction the kraken causes is enough to ruin the town. Even if some of the fleet is saved, the loss of the rest of the vessels is more than Ostin can bear. With the damage the bandits cause, this could well mean the end for Ostin. The mayor will not be able to pay the characters what is owed them, nor will the town be able to support them for more than another week. In all likelihood, Ostin is finished. All that is left is revenge, for which there is no coin to pay but plenty of blood to shed instead.

OSTIN
N
1 Square - 20 Feet
1
2
3
4
5
6
7
8
8
9
10
11
12
13
14
15
16
17
18
19
20
21
22

PART TWO: TROUBLE IN OSTIN

Ostin is a small out-of-the-way fishing village on the Wievin Strip. Even so, it is the largest settlement along that coast and the center for fishing and trade in the southern reaches of Kadalon Bay. The townsfolk are honest, hardworking, and frightened. Not only are the attacks threatening their lives and those of their loved ones, but also, if the grulin run is stopped, the town surely will die. No one in town wants to end up as refugees with no home, no future, and no hope.

OSTIN RUMORS AND LOOSE TALK

The people of Ostin like to gossip, but much of what they talk about in the market and taverns is just that, so much talk. Some clues and bits of wisdom can be found here and there, but a character can also attempt to gain information by talking to people. What individuals know is listed in their descriptions. For general information gathering, roll 1d20 on the table below and give the characters all the information with a target number equal to or lower than the number rolled:

OSTIN RUMORS AND LOOSE TALK TABLE

d20	Rumor/Loose Talk
1	The village of Fadrid was burned to the ground and its people killed. Bandits did it, the same bandits who are plaguing the Bay Road.
2	A ship was seen about two months ago putting into the old harbor on Tern Island. Probably just guano hunters.
3	The baroness went mad after her son died. She even closed the temple to Quell!
4	Bandits are plaguing the Bay Road. Look out or they'll rob you.
5	Sahuagin raids are increasing. They probably have a base underwater or on one of the islands.
6	Ghosts of past priests haunt the old Stormwall Temple.
7	Moon Island is home to all manner of deadly things; no one with a right mind goes there.
8	We've heard strange sounds and seen strange lights out on Bull Island.
9	The Bel'virs dabbled in witchcraft and heresy, and got burned for it.
10	Kaltran Bel'vir was no good and fled before the witch finder came. He left his folks to die.
11	There have been lights in Stormwall Temple, lights where there shouldn't be any.
12	The old blind priest and her apprentice left Stormwall Temple when it was closed and moved to a shack on the Hook.
13	The kraken is just part of the problem. Boats have been found at sea with no living soul on them.
14	Lots of the poor folk on the Hook have fallen sick with a wasting disease.
15	One Bel'vir is left: Kel's sister Sana over in Green Hill. Some say she is a witch like her brother and nephew.
16	The village of Canaada is building a militia; they plan to resist the Oceanics.
17	Baroness Husbridge is planning to hire a private army to take care of the kraken. That won't end well.
18	The baroness and her priest Fellblow looted Stormwall Temple. Quell's wrath is bringing the kraken down upon us.
19	Tern Island is nothing but rocks and birds, that and the old Hyperborean fort.
20	Shell Island? A fine place to stop and eat lunch before coming home with your catch.

OSTIN AND ITS ENVIRONS

Ostin is a small fishing town, but it is the largest of the many fishing settlements along the Wievin Strip. It is home to 1,500 people, mostly humans of Foerdewaith descent, but a few dwarves and half-elves live there as well. It is a peaceful and unchanging town, but one that is beginning to feel the grip of the chaos spreading across the Sundered Kingdoms. The people have watched the advance of the Kingdom of Oceanus with great trepidation, as well as the spread of heretical cults to the south.

Even so, Ostin is still a prosperous town. While there is less traffic along the Bay Road and on Kadalon Bay, the fishing is still good and the grulin run is expected to draw in wealth and visitors as it always has. The local noble, Baroness Husbridge, might be a little too beholden to her priest-sergeant confessor Kas Fellblow and the Church of Mithras, but can any noble rule be called perfect?

O-1. THE HOOKED HAND

Sitting at the base of the Hook where the spur joins the mainland, the Hooked Hand is the lesser of the two inns that serve Ostin. Most of the clientele are common travelers making the journey along the Sea Road to or from Coburn and High Reach. Recent depredations by Oceanic soldiery has limited much of the travel along the road, but the proprietors of the Hooked Hand still turn a fair trade. Six common rooms are upstairs, each with a large rag-stuffed bed. The Hooked Hand does not offer stabling, but instead directs patrons to Bartlett and Bartlett (**Area O-7**) in town.

The inn's common room is the favorite drinking place for the fisherfolk of the town and has a nautical flair. Outsiders are not often welcomed, but neither are they turned away. While the hosts serve ale and fish stew to any who come in, as well as willingly let them rooms, the other patrons tend to keep away from strangers. The local patrons are happy to stand a drink or two for fellow maritime folk with outlandish tales.

HOOKED HAND BILL OF FARE

Item	Cost
Food	
Ale, local	4 cp
Fish stew with bread	3 sp
Roast mutton with leeks, potatoes, and turnips	6 sp
Lodging	
Private room	5 sp/night, includes a meal
Common room	3 sp/night

O-2. THE HOOK

The inner arch of the peninsula protects the cottages and shacks that line the shore, but the ground here is boggy and prone to mudslides from farther up the slope. A small number of shacks belonging to the desperately poor run along the ridge. The people of the Hook are a sad lot and generally rather insular, even from the rest of the people of Ostin. They do not take kindly to strangers poking around in their affairs and might form an angry mob of **2d8 commoners** if the characters behave poorly.

Commoners, Male and Female Humans (2d8): HD 3 each; **AC** 9[10]; **Atk** club (1d4); **Move** 12; **Save** 18; **AL** Any; **CL/XP** B/10; **Special:** none. (*Monstrosities* 254)

Most people who live near the shore of the Hook own short docks and small skiffs or rowboats. A few ply the coast fishing, crabbing, and oystering to make some kind of a living. Their catches are rarely large enough or of high-enough quality for packing in salt to sell to the cities to the north or west, but they do fetch a few coppers on the streets of Ostin.

The last two priests of Stormwall Temple retired to an abandoned cottage on the Hook where they eke out what little living they can to secretly administer to the needs of the fisherfolk, though they always claim they have given up their former vocations. The leader, **Wave Mistress Harfi**, is nearly 90 and almost blind, but her deft fingers still find work mending nets and occasionally using her god-granted powers to heal the sick and injured. She can be found outside of her cottage on most days enjoying the salt breeze and working on broken nets.

Her apprentice, **Wave Tender Kros**, does most of the heavy labor around the cottage. When he can get away, he works on fishing boats for a few days but always hurries back to take care of the elder priest. The two managed to save some of the temple's archives before it was closed; Priest-Sergeant Fellblow burned the rest. They are aware of the ritual to awaken the Island that Dreams and have the real *crown of the master of the island* (see **Appendix B: New Magic Items**) hidden in their cottage. The crown is one of the required items (along with a scepter and toga) that are needed to complete the ritual. If approached peacefully and convinced of the characters' good intentions, they might help awaken the Island that Dreams to fight the kraken.

Wave Tender Harfi, Female Human Priestess of Quell (Clr8):
HP 33; AC 9[10]; Atk none; Move 12; Save 8; AL L; CL/XP 9/1100; Special: +2 save versus paralyzation and poison, banish undead, spells (2/2/2/2/2).
Spells: 1st—*cure light wounds* (x2); 2nd—*bless, speak with animals*; 3rd—*cure disease, prayer*; 4th—*create water, cure serious wounds*; 5th—*commune, create food*.

Wave Tender Kros, Male Human Priest of Quell (Clr4): HP 18; AC 5[14]; Atk mace (1d6); Move 12; Save 12; AL L; CL/XP 5/240; Special: +2 save versus paralyzation and poison, banish undead, spells (2/1).
Spells: 1st—*cure light wounds, purify food and drink*; 2nd—*bless*.
Equipment: chainmail, mace, 1d4 sp.

O-3. The Slough

This boggy wetland is a low point where water from the bay flows in during high tide and storms. The Bay Road crosses the mouth of the Slough on a newly repaired stone bridge, and the town has a low sea wall built along the eastern edge of the Slough to prevent flooding from that direction. This area does not have any appreciable standing water, but it is sandy, marshy, and a general wasteland.

O-4. Docks

The pride of Ostin is its fishing fleet, which ties up to the town's main docks. Each fisherfolk family owns a dock and usually the boats tied up there, but a few slips are left open for visiting vessels. The harbor is deep, deep enough to accept big ocean-going caravels and cogs. The waters around the docks are filled with scavenging fish, with the occasional **shark** nosing around.

**Medium Shark: HD 5; AC 6[13]; Atk bite (1d6+2); Move 0 (swim 24); Save 12; AL N; CL/XP 5/240; Special: feeding frenzy (1-in-6 chance to attack another shark). (*Monstrosities* 420)

O-5. Boardwalk

The Bay Road ends just after the flood control barrier that blocks the Slough from the town and becomes a well-maintained boardwalk along the docks, which are raised on stone piers above the water. The shops and homes facing the boardwalk connect to it and form a long wall of buildings along its entire length. The Bay Road resumes its muddy way toward the Matagost Peninsula just past the row of easternmost buildings.

O-6. Raymond's Chandler Shop

Depending on the time of year and what fish are running, the fleet of vessels out of Ostin fish the mornings, afternoons, or overnight. Even during the day, storms can cause the light to fade, and thus having good lighting aboard ship is paramount. Raymond is a third-generation chandler, and his family has owned this shop for more than a century. He makes candles, lanterns, and other light sources, but is best known for making storm- and wave-proof lanterns that do not risk setting a boat on fire. He also dabbles in other combustibles and makes fireworks for signal rockets and entertainment. A stormproof lantern is a metal hooded lantern that is not easily extinguished by the wind or even brief submersion in water. The lantern costs 10 gp. Fireworks in a variety of colors can be purchased as well for 8 sp a rocket.

**Raymond, Male Dwarf Chandler: HP 6; AC 9[10]; Atk dagger (1d4); Move 9; Save 18; AL L; CL/XP B/10; Special: +4 save vs. magic, darkvision (60ft), detect stonework. (*Monstrosities* 254)

O-7. Bartlett and Bartlett

Sunderland is known for its horses, and along the Wievin Strip, Bartlett and Bartlett are known as the best horse traders, furriers, and breeders. The twin sisters maintain a small ranch outside Ostin but dwell behind their livery stable at the north edge of town. Katti and Matti are two husky women who have spent their long lives working with horses, including shodding, treating ailments and injuries, and breaking mounts. They brook no nonsense and do not suffer fools lightly, but they do know their horses.

**Katti Bartlett, Female Human: HP 14; AC 9[10]; Atk whip (1d4); Move 12; Save 16; AL L; CL/XP 2/30; Special: none. (*Monstrosities* 254)

**Matti Bartlett, Female Human: HP 16; AC 9[10]; Atk staff (1d6); Move 12; Save 16; AL L; CL/XP 2/30; Special: none. (*Monstrosities* 254)

Bartlett and Bartlett Bill of Services

Service	Price
Stabling	8 cp/day
Shoeing	1 gp/hoof
Tack and harness repair	1–9 sp
Wagon or cart repair	1–15 gp
Healing (horses only)	varies by ailment
Horse rental	5 gp/day
Riding horse*	100 gp
Warhorse*	600 gp

* These horses are some of the best in Sunderland and have maximum hit points. They are well trained; riders have advantage on rolls to control their mounts.

O-8. Mary's Tackle

Old Mary is really not that old as far as elves go, but to the people of Ostin she is an ancient being who sold tackle and nets to their great-grandparents. She makes all of her goods herself and often has a long waiting list for net repairs or special orders (the fisherfolk are always dreaming up new and improved fishing tackle). She gets the raw rope and metal parts from various sources around town, and she often employs the people of the Hook or retired fisherfolk as net menders. She has a lot of rope at her shop and could conceivably build something that could hook and hold a kraken, provided a ship large enough not to be dragged down by it or a person strong enough to reel it in exists.

**Old Mary, Female Elf Net Mender: HP 5; AC 9[10]; Atk dagger (1d4); Move 12; Save 18; AL L; CL/XP B/10; Special: darkvision (60ft), detect secret doors. (*Monstrosities* 254)

O-9. The Salmon and Shark

Better-off travelers and those with sensitive tastes are directed to the Salmon and Shark, Ostin's best inn. While the Hooked Hand manages to keep afloat by serving the local fisherfolk watered-down ale and fish stew, the Salmon is barely managing to get by on what little trade comes down the road or sails into port. The grulin run brings in merchants from across the Sundered Kingdoms and Borderland Provinces who spend enough coin to maintain the inn through the rest of the year.

The characters are housed here as long as they are in good graces with the town and the mayor. The bar and kitchen are open, and the characters are put up in one of the inn's 12 private rooms (though not the two royal rooms unless a character carries a patent or other sign of nobility). If they abuse this service, the mayor hears about it and is less than cordial in dealing with any other slights the characters happen to inflict.

Drink	
Ale, local	6 cp
Ale, Oestre Red	7 cp
Ale, Endhome Dark	7 cp
Wine, per bottle	10 gp
Dwarven whiskey	5 gp
Other spirits	1 gp
Food	
Cheese, fruit, and nuts	4 sp
Roast mutton with potatoes, leeks, and onions	6 sp
Roast pork with mushrooms and onions	8 sp
Salmon fillet with rice	2 gp
Shark steak with potatoes	5 gp
Lodging	
Private room (feather bed, locked chest)	8 sp
Royal room (locked doors, locked chest, feather bed)	5 gp

O-10. Town Plaza

The pride of Ostin is its plaza, a large paved area in the center of town that serves as a common meeting place for the townsfolk. It is the site of the weekly market that brings in farmers and fisherfolk from across the Wievin Strip. A large marble fountain at the center of the plaza once boasted a statue of the sea god Quell, but it now is empty of any decoration or water. The witch hunter Jarlitha the Pious ordered the fountain drained so she could erect a post for the burning of witches and heretics. The baroness removed the statue during her purge of the worship of Quell. The Bel'virs were burned here, and the townsfolk have carefully avoided the fountain ever since, not even bothering to clean the burn marks off the stone.

O-11. Mayor's House

Sitting on High Street across the square from St. Matta's is a well-maintained three-story house. The main parts of the exterior are painted dark green, while the molding is done in blue, red, and yellow. The effect is rather garish, made even more so by the excessive use of ornamental plants and decorations. This is the house of the current mayor of Ostin, and indeed was the home of three previous mayors, all of whom came from the respectable if eccentric Horsby family.

The interior is just as baroquely provincial and bourgeoisie as the outside, which suits **Mayor Horsby** just fine. In addition to his wife **Matilia** and three children, Jasitlia (see below), 18-year-old **Marud**, and 12-year-old **Brucilia**, the mayor employs a live-in maid named **Conilia**, **Drus** the gardener, and allows the 12-year-old orphan boy **Haliti** to sleep in the kitchen when he is not running errands for his excellency.

If the characters are chased out of both inns and are still in the mayor's good graces, he puts them up at his house. The food is plentiful but average, and the mayor is not much of a drinker other than small beer. The house is not large enough to take on more than three guests, so there likely will be some sharing of rooms.

Mayor Horsby, Male Human: HP 12; AC 9[10]; Atk none; Move 12; Save 16; AL L; CL/XP 2/30; Special: none. (*Monstrosities* 254)

Matilia Horsby, Female Half-Elf: HP 4; AC 9[10]; Atk none; Move 12; Save 18; AL L; CL/XP B/10; Special: darkvision (60ft). (*Monstrosities* 254)

Marud Horsby, Male Human Acolyte (Clr1): HP 4; AC 9[10]; Atk mace (1d6); Move 12; Save 15; AL L; CL/XP 1/15; Special: +2 save versus paralyzation and poison, banish undead. Equipment: mace

Brucilia Horsby, Female Human: HP 4; AC 9[10]; Atk none; Move 12; Save 18; AL L; CL/XP B/10; Special: none. (*Monstrosities* 254)

Conilia, Female Human Maid: HP 3; AC 9[10]; Atk rolling pin (1d4); Move 12; Save 18; AL Any; CL/XP B/10; Special: none. (*Monstrosities* 254)

Drus, Male Human Gardener: HP 5; AC 9[10]; Atk club (1d4); Move 12; Save 18; AL Any; CL/XP B/10; Special: none. (*Monstrosities* 254)

Haliti, Male Human Orphan: HP 2; AC 9[10]; Atk none; Move 12; Save 18; AL Any; CL/XP B/10; Special: none. (*Monstrosities* 254)

The eldest child of Mayor Horsby, **Jasitlia Horsby** is a 20-year-old woman living a double life. By day, she is the dutiful daughter of the mayor, educated, well-dressed, and courteous. She attends most of her father's meetings and appears to be the perfect successor should she avoid scandal, marry well, and if the baroness selects her.

When the moon is full, she dons leather armor and arms herself with a sword and dagger. She slips out of her father's house and takes the Bay Road, where she meets with a few likeminded sons and daughters of the elite of Ostin. They waylay merchants and other travelers for sport, to commit petty robberies of farmsteads, to steal horses to ride around with reckless abandon, to overturn boats, and sometimes simply to intimidate strangers for laughs. So far, they have not killed anyone and have managed to keep their depredations a secret. However, the orphan errand-boy Haliti who sleeps in the kitchen of the mayor's house has seen Jasitlia coming and going at night and knows her secret.

Jasitlia Horsby, Bandit Leader: HP 21; **AC** 7[12]; **Atk** short sword (1d6) or dagger (1d4); **Move** 12; **Save** 13; **AL** N; **CL/XP** 4/120; **Special:** none. (*Monstrosities* 254)
Equipment: leather armor, short sword, dagger, 1d6 sp.

O-12. NEW TEMPLE

This building used to be the old temple dedicated to a range of gods the people of Ostin saw as less important than Quell. The baroness ordered it partially demolished and rebuilt as a temple to Mithras last year. The work had barely begun when many of the stonemasons fled after the kraken started attacking. All that stands now is a stone shell and framework.

O-13. HASTRIDGE HOUSE

The home of the Hastridge family, this stone and timber building is in good repair and shows the signs of a prosperous but tasteful fisherfolk family. The Hastridges are one of the preeminent fishing families in Ostin, owning three ships and a four-slip dock. They were one of the most strident voices to condemn the Bel'virs during their trial and benefited greatly from the sale of the Bel'virs' properties at bargain rates.

An old traditionalist family, the Hastridges maintain a secret shrine to Quell in their basement. Wave Tender Kros comes here weekly and on holy days to perform services for the small congregation, and to secretly bless the fleet before it goes out to sea at the start of each season. If found out, it is likely that the baroness comes down hard on the Hastridges, possibly even bringing in a witch hunter to declare them and Kos as heretics of some sort.

O-14. TOWER HOUSE

Home for 10 generations of the Hightower family, Tower House is a stone and wood building with a tall, narrow tower rising from its seaward side. The house is prosperous, though not ostentatiously so, and the Hightower family is known for its solid members — good fishing boat captains all — and a certain luck when it comes to finding schools of fish in the deep ocean.

The scion of this distinguished family is the feckless and often confused **Eso Hightower**. Eso is the leader of the actual cult of Kunulo the Hungering Tide in Ostin, though that cult numbers only him and three other well-off scions of prominent families. In his youth, Eso was friendly with Kaltran, if only because he found the sorcerer's weird ways to be intriguing. With Kaltran returned, Eso now acts as his spy in Ostin and sends daily reports at night via his bat familiar.

Eso is no threat by himself, and even with his **3 cultist minions**, he is not much of an encounter. However, he can see the entire town from his tower and tracks the characters' movements, whom they speak with, and what they do. His minions loiter about near the characters when possible, eavesdrop on them at inns, and pay off servants to find out more information. If confronted, Eso fights. If reduced to fewer than half his hit points, he surrenders and tells the characters of Kaltran's plans and where the sorcerer acquired the kraken summoning ritual.

Eso Hightower, Male Human Cultist of Kunulo the Hungering Tide (Clr3): HP 14; **AC** 7[12]; **Atk** mace (1d6); **Move** 12; **Save** 13; **AL** C; **CL/XP** 3/60; **Special:** +2 save versus paralyzation and poison, banish undead, spells (2).
Spells: 1st—*cause light wounds* (x2).
Equipment: leather armor, mace.
Cultists, Male or Female Humans (3): HD 1; **HP** 7, 5, 4; **AC** 7[12]; **Atk** daggers (1d4); **Move** 12; **Save** 17; **AL** C; **CL/XP** 1/15; **Special:** none. (*Monstrosities* 254)

PART THREE: THE WIEVIN STRIP

The southern stretch of Kadalon Bay from Cobrun to where the Matagost Peninsula turns the shore of the bay northward is known as the Wievin Strip. The great plains and grasslands of central Sunderland roll to the sea unimpeded by mountains or hills, indeed by even forests. It is a windswept expanse of shoreline dotted with small fishing villages, crude baronies, and tiny coves that all too often are the haunts of pirates and smugglers.

WIEVIN STRIP RANDOM ENCOUNTERS

The following encounters occur whenever the characters are traveling the Wievin Strip either along the Bay Road or inland through the ranches and farmland. Due to the nature of the terrain, inland encounters occur at around half a mile; on the road, sand dunes block sight inland and the curve of the coast restricts sightlines to a quarter mile or less. Even so, most of the time characters will not be surprised or ambushed unless otherwise noted.

Check for encounters once every hour of travel, or every six hours if stationary.

d100	Encounter
01–30	No encounter
31–40	Merchants
41–50	Bandits?
51–60	Manticores
61–70	Fisherfolk
71–80	Herd of Horses
81–90	Sahuagin Raid
91–100	Oceanic Soldiers

Bandits? These are not true bandits, just Jasitlia and a band of eight youths from Ostin. They do not attack but prefer to instead ride up with cloaked faces to intimidate travelers. They do not have the stomach for a fight, for in reality they are simply privileged bullies out causing mayhem for fun. If attacked, half of them fight back for a round before fleeing; the others flee at the first opportunity. They do not pose a serious threat to a prepared party of adventurers, but the real challenge is if any of the "bandits" is injured, or worse, killed. Explaining to the mayor why the scions of the town's greatest families were attacked on the road is difficult.

Jasitlia Horsby, Bandit Leader: HP 21; **AC** 7[12]; **Atk** short sword (1d6) or dagger (1d4); **Move** 12; **Save** 13; **AL** N; **CL/XP** 4/120; **Special:** none. (*Monstrosities* 254)

Equipment: leather armor, short sword, dagger, 1d6 sp.

"Bandits," Male or Female Youths (8): HD 4 each; **AC** 9[10]; **Atk** short sword (1d6); **Move** 12; **Save** 18; **AL** Any; **CL/XP** B/10; **Special:** none. (*Monstrosities* 254)

Fisherfolk. This group of **2d6 fisherfolk** are simply traveling along the road. There is a 2-in-6 chance that they were attacked by Jasitlia's bandits and beaten up, but oddly not robbed.

Fisherfolk, Male or Female Humans (2d6): HD 1d6hp; **AC** 9[10]; **Atk** weapon (1d6); **Move** 12; **Save** 18; **AL** Any; **CL/XP** B/10; **Special:** none. (*Monstrosities* 254)

Herd of Horses. This large herd of 2d100 horses is being driven to market in Coburn. Their herders are leery of strangers but not unfriendly. However, the horses block travel along the path or road for an hour. The herd has a 1-in-8 chance to panic and stampede out of control, creating a dangerous situation as the characters must face down tons of frightened horseflesh.

Manticores. This pair of mated manticores roosts in the rocky islands offshore, where they spend their days hunting fish, livestock, and stray humanoids. They do not attack a large or armed party. They hover well above bow range and watch interesting movement through the area for 2d6 hours. These creatures are best used to cause tension and as a handy excuse to stampede horses. If another encounter occurs, the manticores swoop in at opportune moments to snatch away the dead and wounded.

Manticores (2): HD 6+4; **AC** 4[15]; **Atk** 2 claws (1d3), bite (1d8), 6 tail spikes (1d6); **Move** 12 (fly 18); **Save** 11; **AL** C; **CL/XP** 8/800; **Special:** tail spikes (6 spikes per round, 180ft range). (*Monstrosities* 316)

Merchants. A merchant wagon trundles by, stopping to exchange news and gossip if the characters appear friendly. There is a 1-in-4 chance that Jasitlia and her bandits roughed up, but didn't rob, the merchants. The bandits let them go after breaking a few of their wares.

Oceanic Soldiers. This patrol of soldiers from the Kingdom of Oceanus is part of that nation's ongoing push out of the Matagost Peninsula and into northern Sunderland. They do not hide who they are and travel with drums beating and banners aflutter. Their mission is to sow fear and to intimidate the locals, as well as to engage and destroy any threatening monsters or bandit groups (this will win hearts and minds, or so their superiors think). The characters might very well look like a prime target, and if so, the soldiers set up an ambush and attack. The patrol is led by a **sergeant** and contains **15 soldiers**.

Oceanic Sergeant, Male or Female Human: HD 3; **AC** 5[14]; **Atk** longsword (1d8); **Move** 12; **Save** 14; **AL** N; **CL/XP** 3/60; **Special:** none. (*Monstrosities* 256)

Oceanic Soldiers, Male or Female Humans (15): HD 1; **AC** 7[12]; **Atk** longsword (1d8); **Move** 12; **Save** 17; **AL** N; **CL/XP** 1/15; **Special:** none. (*Monstrosities* 257)

Sahuagin Raid. The Kingdom of Oceanus is not the only foreign power that sees the chaos and lack of a centralized government in Sunderland as an opportunity. This raiding party of **2d8 + 3 sahuagin** has come ashore to sow chaos, commit murder, and loot. They come out of the sea to ambush travelers along the Bay Road and disappear back into the sea afterward.

Sahuagins (2d8+3): HD 2+1; **AC** 5[14]; **Atk** weapon (1d8); **Move** 12 (swim 18); **Save** 16; **AL** C; **CL/XP** 2/30; **Special:** none. (*Monstrosities* 407)

Bastin

This small farming village has a population of around 300 people, mostly humans, but a few half-elves live here as well. The village grows wheat, barley, and millet, and small vegetable plots can be found behind nearly every house. Soldiers from the Oceanic-controlled settlements to the west come every fall to take half of the produce as "taxes," but their patrols are not yet frequent enough to keep away monsters wandering down from the Matagost Range to the southeast. As a result, the once-prosperous villagers are becoming impoverished. A mated pair of **owlbears** has been seen stalking the grasslands, along with other beasts.

Owlbears (2): HD 5+1; **HP** 37, 33; **AC** 5[14]; **Atk** 2 claws (1d6), bite (2d6); **Move** 12; **Save** 12; **AL** N; **CL/XP** 5/240; **Special:** hug (additional 2d8 if to-hit roll is 18+). (*Monstrosities* 368)

Bay Road

Running from Coburn to Highreach, the Bay Road runs along the southern edge of Kadalon Bay and up the northern coast of the Matagost Peninsula. It once was a moderately well-traveled road serving the numerous small finishing villages and towns along the bay as well as nearby farms and ranches. Last summer, the Oceanic army began to impose its control over the eastern end of the road, reducing travel and making everyone from Matagost to the Wievin Strip nervous.

The road has not been well maintained but the bridges are still intact, even if the cobblestones that once covered its length are largely washed out or overgrown. For long stretches, the road is not much more than two wagon ruts cutting along through the prairie that grows nearly to the seashore. Around larger towns such as Ostin are several miles of good road, along which patrols maintain a watch for bandits and monsters.

Where the road crosses small streams, there may or may not be a bridge, but the bridge over the Wievin River is intact. Baroness Husbridge established a small guardhouse with **3 guards** on watch who collect a copper for every person who crosses the bridge and a silver for every horse. In places, the Bay Road runs a mile or more inland behind tall sand dunes. In other places where the coastline is rockier or the ground firmer, the road runs just above the high-tide mark.

Guards, Male or Female Humans (3): HD 1; **HP** 6 each; **AC** 7[12]; **Atk** longsword (1d8); **Move** 12; **Save** 17; **AL** N; **CL/XP** 1/15; **Special:** none. (*Monstrosities* 257)

Bull Island

More than a sandbar but less than a true island, Bull Island is largely submerged during storms but manages to rise a dozen feet out of the sea the rest of the time. Local sailors know it well, for the island is surrounded by a deceptive sandbar that often looks to be deep water from a distance, but turns out to be only a few feet of freeboard as one approaches. A small band of **14 sahuagin** has set up a base here using the ephemeral nature of the island and its large sandbar to allow them to store items that are best kept out of the water, such as six captives, while maintaining their own submerged living spaces.

Sahuagins (14): HD 2+1; **AC** 5[14]; **Atk** weapon (1d8); **Move** 12 (swim 18); **Save** 16; **AL** C; **CL/XP** 2/30; **Special:** none. (*Monstrosities* 407)

Canaada

This small farming village is much like those found across Sunderland Province. The village is home to 250 villagers, all humans, who spend their days growing wheat, corn, and alfalfa. The villagers are closely related to those in Sand Briar and keep close tabs on what is going on with the fisherfolk of the Wievin Strip.

On the surface, Canaada is a quiet farming community like so many others found inland along the Wievin Strip. However, the people are beginning to fear the encroaching power of the Kingdom of Oceanus. They have stockpiled a small amount of arms and armor and plan to mount a defense. However, they are farmers and not warriors. What they really need is for someone to train them in the arts of war, or better yet, to talk some sense into them for they do not stand a chance against professional soldiers.

Estvin Ranch

This sprawling ranch raises some of the finest horses in Sunderland, and certainly the finest horses along the Wievin Strip. The heart of the ranch is a sprawling walled homestead containing a barn, a bunkhouse, outbuildings, and a main house. The Estvin family is the second wealthiest family in the strip and could easily challenge the baroness for sheer economic and martial might. In addition to **Sir Karl Estivin** and his two wives, 13 children (half of whom are adults), two siblings and their families, the ranch employs 20 farmhands of various types, most to work the herds. All told, in time of need the ranch can supply eight mounted and armored warriors as well as an additional dozen armored men-at-arms and six archers. Normally, these are employed to guard the herds and to patrol the ranch's sprawling lands to keep out rustlers, bandits, and monsters. The baroness can call upon this levy as well, but in practice she does not push her luck with the independent-minded Sir Estivin.

Sir Karl Estivin, Male Human Knight (Ftr6): HP 42; AC 4[15];
   Atk longsword (1d8+1); **Move** 12; **Save** 9; **AL** L; **CL/XP** 6/400;
   Special: +1 to hit and damage strength bonus, multiple attacks (6) vs. creatures with 1 or fewer HD.
Equipment: chainmail, shield, longsword.

Fadird

The small fishing village of Fadird was burned to the ground a month before the kraken attacks started. There were no survivors and no witnesses; the people of the Wievin Strip assumed that bandits or Oceanic soldiers were to blame, as well as more outlandish ideas. The truth is that Kaltran tested the kraken's abilities on the unsuspecting village of Fadird.

Green Hill

The largest and most prosperous of the farming villages of the Wievin Strip, Green Hill sits on a lightly wooded hill surrounded by the Sunderland grasslands. It is unwalled and has nearly 800 residents. There is a smithy, a stable, and a few merchants and crafts folk. The big business for the village is the annual Horse Fair that sees herds brought in from deep in the Sunderland, as well as merchants from across the Sundered Kingdoms and Borderland Provinces.

Sana Bel'vir and her wife **Jisa** live in Green Hill. Sana is Kaltran's aunt and knows the story of her nephew's problems, his flight from home, his years adventuring, and the murder of her brother and sister-in-law. Sana is a saddler and horse trader with strong contacts in the rancher community, especially with her old friend Sir Estivin. She is hesitant to speak of her nephew or her brother's death, but her wife is more than willing to talk to friendly adventurers who want to help.

Sana Bel'vir, Female Human: HP 17; AC 9[10]; **Atk** whip
   (1d4); **Move** 12; **Save** 14; **AL** N; **CL/XP** 3/60; **Special:** none.
   (*Monstrosities* 254)
Jisa, Female Half-Elf, Female Human: HP 4; AC 9[10]; **Atk** none;
   Move 12; **Save** 18; **AL** Any; **CL/XP** B/10; **Special:** darkvision (60ft).
   (*Monstrosities* 254)

The Hook

This low peninsula juts out into Kadalon Bay and provides the protection that allows Ostin to have a safe and well-shielded harbor. A high ridge runs along the center of the peninsula but its steep slopes leave little purchase for buildings save those close to the waterline. A broken road runs from the Bay Road out to the tip of the peninsula and the abandoned Stormwall Temple dedicated to the sea god Quell.

Husbridge Keep

The only fortification along the Wievin Strip, Husbridge Keep is a square motte-and-bailey castle on an artificial hill next to the Wievin River. The river has been partially diverted to fill a moat. A wooden palisade surrounds the keep and extends to protect the far side of the bridge that crosses the moat. Across the river from Husbridge Keep is the village of Vilatin where the peasants sworn to the Husbridges live and work.

The keep is a small affair and houses the baroness, her priest confessor Fellblow, and her small entourage of servants and men-at-arms. Her stables house only a half dozen war mounts, but nearly a dozen riding horses from the Estivin Ranch (her annual tax, which she resells as needed).

Kadalon Bay

Framed by the Matagost Peninsula to the east and the Sand Hills to the west, Kadalon Bay is an extension of the Sinnar Ocean. Most shipping journeys to Coburn to the west of the Wievin Strip, leaving the fishing boats of Ostin and its neighboring villages free to chase their catches.

Moon Island

Named for its crescent shape, Moon Island is regularly avoided by the local fisherfolk. Legends say that the island is cursed and haunted; those who travel there are never heard from again. Many of the fisherfolk say it is dangerous to even approach the island, though some good fishing spots are nearby that the foolish or bold will troll. The prevalence of good fishing around the island likely has more to do with the fact that most of the fisherfolk leave it alone rather than anything supernatural, but tongues do wag.

The island is home to a large population of rats, including several **giant rats** and a small clan of **wererats**. These isolated degenerates have interbred with each other and the rats of the island for generations. They are even more feral and untrustworthy than their mainland relatives. The few visitors who brave the legends of Moon Island are attacked by the hordes of rats and eaten.

Wererat: HD 3; AC 6[13]; **Atk** bite (1d3), weapon (1d6); **Move** 12;
   Save 14; **AL** C; **CL/XP** 4/120; **Special:** +1 or better magic or silver
   weapons to hit, control rats, lycanthropy, surprise (1–4 on 1d6).
   (*Monstrosities* 307)
Giant Rat: HD 1d4 hp; AC 7[12]; **Atk** bite (1d3); **Move** 12; **Save** 18;
   AL N; **CL/XP** A/5; **Special:** 5% are diseased. (*Monstrosities* 384)

Ostin

Ostin is detailed in **Part Two: Trouble in Ostin**.

Sand Briar

Unlike the other fishing villages along the Wievin Strip, Sand Briar sits in the sea on stilts and focuses more on clams and other shellfish than deep-sea fishing. The village is in the middle of a large mudflat that floods at high tide and is left as a wet morass at low tide. The locals harvest the many clams, oysters, and mussels found in the mud flats, smoke them using peat from nearby bogs, and then pack them in salt for shipping to Ostin and then on to foreign ports.

The village is governed by a council of elders, as is common in the area, but also venerates and sacrifices to Marie le Diable, a **bog hag** and her **3 bog beast** sons. She keeps **6 bog zombies** in her lair, but the bog beasts roam about a bit (35% chance of 1d3 in her lair). Every full moon, the villagers take a selection of foodstuffs and alcohol to a standing stone in the bog and leave it. Once every lunar year, they must bring a human sacrifice to Marie le Diable. This is usually a traveler or other stranger, but when one cannot be found, the villagers draw lots to determine who will be that year's victim.

Marie le Diable, Bog Hag: HD 7; HP 48; AC 2[17]; **Atk** 2 claws
   (2d4 + poison); **Move** 12 (swim 12); **Save** 9; **AL** C; **CL/XP** 11/1700;
   Special: +1 or better magic weapons to hit, create bog zombie (slain
   victims rise within 7 days), darkvision (60ft), immune to poison,
   magic resistance (10%), poison (save or flesh rots, 1d6 damage
   per day until healed), resist cold and fire (50% damage), spell-like
   abilities. (See **Appendix A: New Monsters**)
   Spell-like abilities: at will—*darkness 15ft radius, phantasmal
   force*; 2/day—*magic missile, polymorph self, suggestion.*
Bog Beasts (3): HD 5; HP 35, 32, 30; AC 5[14]; **Atk** 2 claws (1d6 +
   swamp fever); **Move** 12; **Save** 12; **AL** N; **CL/XP** 6/400; **Special:**
   rend (additional 2d6 damage if both claws hit target), swamp fever
   (movement halved, −2 penalty to AC and saves; −2 save each day to
   resist disease). (*The Tome of Horrors Complete* 65)
Bog Zombies (6): HD 3; HP 21, 19x2, 16, 15, 10; AC 7[12]; **Atk** strike
   (1d8); **Move** 6 (swim 9); **Save** 14; **AL** N; **CL/XP** 3/60; **Special:**
   immune to sleep and charm, stench (10ft radius, save or −1 to hit
   and damage), vulnerable to fire (200% damage). (See **Appendix A:
   New Monsters**)

Shell Island

Shell Island is not the grass-covered, steep-sided island that the locals have always known. It is actually the shell of a sleeping dragon turtle placed into a dreaming state by the power of the priesthood of Quell millennia ago. As the great beast has bobbed along in the sea, barnacles and other accretions have formed on its body, anchoring it to the sea floor in Kadalon Bay. Likewise, soil accumulated on its massive shell, providing solid footing for grasses to grow. Many of the local fisherfolk are known to stop at Shell Island while fishing to cook their lunch before heading back home with the day's catch.

Stormwall Temple

This ancient temple to the sea god Quell was built during the height of the Hyperborean Empire. It has long been in decline and was officially closed three years ago by the baroness on advice from her confessor Priest-Sergeant Fellblow. It is detailed in **Part Four: Stormwall Temple**.

Tern Island

A Hyperborean fortress once stood on this rocky island, guarding the sea lanes that ran by the Wievin Strip. Like so many fortresses, the one on Tern Island was abandoned when the empire fell. Today, it is a ruined stump and the island is mostly known for the flocks of seabirds that roost there. More information on Tern Island can be found in **Part Five: Tern Island**.

Vilatin

This squat village of huts and thatch roofs serves as Husbridge Keep. The peasants here have long been pledged to the Husbridge family and despite the poverty they live in, they are known for their loyalty to the baroness. They work her fields and herd her livestock, and in return, they receive her protection and occasional beneficence. The highest desire of many in the village is to be chosen to serve in the keep where they receive better quarters, food, and clothing, as well as the respect of their peers.

Wievin River

The lazy waters of the Wievin River wind their way to Kaladan Bay through grasslands, farms, and ranches. The river is rarely high enough to float a barge of any significant size, something that has limited the development of the Wievin Strip. Its banks are low and often break to form small bogs and marshes. In places, it is hard to tell where the river ends and the wetlands begin.

PART FOUR: STORMWALL TEMPLE

Built by the long-dead Hyperborean Empire, Stormwall Temple served the followers of the sea god Quell for millennia. Three years ago, under the advice of her confessor Priest-Sergeant Fellblow, Baroness Husbridge ordered the temple closed and its priesthood sent away. Since that time, the temple has been experiencing a long period of decay, for although the fisherfolk of the Wievin Strip were regular patrons, they were never wealthy enough to provide more than minimal maintenance of the sprawling complex. The priests once numbered more than a hundred, but by the time it was closed, only two priests were living at the temple. Both retired to the small fishing village of Fadird where they remain in retirement.

HISTORY OF STORMWALL TEMPLE

Built during the last century of the Hyperborean Empire, Stormwall Temple displays the heights of engineering and art that the culture was known for, as well as the lax standards of the last years of the empire. The temple is decorated with reliefs, statues, and carved adornments. The walls rise high into the sky upon solid foundations. A central spire extends above the altar and once held intricate stained glass.

However, much of the temple is not made from dressed and cut stone but concrete, and poor concrete at that. Many areas leak in the rain or have partially collapsed under the weight of time and weather. Even when a full priesthood served here, there was never enough wealth or manpower to maintain the entire temple to the degree it deserved.

After the empire fell, the temple was left to its own devices. At times it was abandoned entirely, only to be rediscovered centuries later. With the coming of the Foerdewaith peoples and the establishment of new settlements along the Wievin Strip, the temple entered a renaissance of sorts. Damaged areas were patched, although to a less-skillful degree using cut stone brought down from the Matagost Mountains, and worn areas were shored up. As the population of the region declined, so too did the prospects for the temple, and the building began to again fall apart.

Three years ago, the temple was shuttered by order of Baroness Husbridge. For some time, the barons of Husbridge had donated to the temple as part of their duties as the local feudal lord, but the Husbridges are an inland family and the seat of their power and wealth is in the grasslands, farms, and ranches of Sunderland, not the fishing villages bordering Kadalon Bay. When the baroness's confessor, Priest-Sergeant Fellblow of Mithras, campaigned to close down all temples, shrines, and congregations worshipping what he termed lesser and failed gods, the baroness saw a chance at a power grab in the region, a bit of looting of temples, and a reason to cut her donations to Stormwall Temple. This move was not popular with the fisherfolk of her demesne, but they had little power to do much more than complain.

The last two priests, Wave Mistress Harfi and her apprentice Wave Tender Kros, were forced to flee the temple, but they gathered a few bits and pieces of the archives in the process. Among the items they salvaged was the *crown of the Island that Dreams* (see **Appendix B: New Magic Items**). Priest-Sergeant Fellblow and the baroness took the remainder of the temple's treasures back to Husbridge with them.

However, the looters and the last priests were unaware of a hidden shrine deep within the temple. This shrine contained the ritual instructions and paraphernalia needed to summon forth a kraken and place it under the ritualist's control. Kaltran Bel'vir discovered the location of the Shrine of the Kraken and the ritual during his adventuring days. After his parents' murder, he returned to loot this hidden room, taking the ritual paraphernalia and copying the ritual before he destroyed the fresco that described it.

Kaltran slew most of the creatures that inhabited the abandoned temple, but others followed after he left. The **3 vampire spawn Belsir of Reme** and his lovers **Tala** and **Tef** took up residence in the temple. They had been fleeing a noted vampire hunter, Raitia of the Bloody Stake, and managed to lose her somewhere in Eastreach. Not taking any chances, they traveled farther south and east to the Sundered Kingdoms. They have been using the temple as a base for only a few months and feeding lightly on the poorer fisherfolk of the Hook or on sailors on boats out at sea. These vampire spawn developed the ability to shapechange into bats and thus can flit across the water to attack fishing boats out on the water at night.

Belsir of Reme, Male Vampire Spawn: HD 5; HP 37; AC 4[15]; Atk bite (1d10); **Move** 12 (fly 18); **Save** 12; **AL** C; **CL/XP** 8/800; **Special:** +1 or better magic weapon to hit, charm gaze (as *charm person*, −1 save), regenerate (1hp/round), shapeshift. (*Monstrosities* 498) **Equipment:** *toga of the master of the Island that Dreams* (see **Appendix B: New Magic Items**).

Tala, Female Vampire Spawn: HD 5; HP 30; AC 4[15]; Atk bite (1d10); **Move** 12 (fly 18); **Save** 12; **AL** C; **CL/XP** 8/800; **Special:** +1 or better magic weapon to hit, charm gaze (as *charm person*, −1 save), regenerate (1hp/round), shapeshift. (*Monstrosities* 498)

Tef, Male Vampire Spawn: HD 5; HP 33; AC 4[15]; Atk bite (1d10); **Move** 12 (fly 18); **Save** 12; **AL** C; **CL/XP** 8/800; **Special:** +1 or better magic weapon to hit, charm gaze (as *charm person*, −1 save), regenerate (1hp/round), shapeshift. (*Monstrosities* 498)

Stormwall Today

Never in great condition, the temple has fallen into a state of disrepair from which it might not recover. Untended these past three years, and only barely looked after by its two remaining priests in the decade before, much of the temple is now in ruin. The grand spire that once served as a watchtower and lighthouse has fallen; its remains lie at the foot of the cliffs upon which the temple stands.

The temple is a rectangular building in the classic late-Hyperborean style with a surrounding double colonnade, peaked roof, open portico, and triangular entablature. The reliefs and other decorations are largely worn away, and all that remains of their paint is a few grayish chips. A closer examination picks out images of the sea god Quell, sea life, and similar motifs, but so little remains that any narrative or symbology the sculptors intended is long gone. The interior is unlit unless otherwise noted and made from stone that always seems slightly damp and slick to the touch.

Approaching the Temple

The temple sits at the end of the Hook where a spur from the Bay Road runs from the base of the peninsula out along the top of the ridge to the plaza fronting the temple. This plaza is now an overgrown 15 acres of broken stone filled with weeds and small trees. A set of steps leads up from the plaza and onto the pronaos.

T-1. Pronaos

This shallow portico separates the outer space from the sacred inner space. Once, mighty bronze doors closed off the portico from the cella, but these have fallen and are covered in verdigris and lichen. A tripwire runs across the empty doorway. If tripped, the wire causes a set of chimes inside the doorway to tinkle to alert the vampire spawn in the sub-basement.

T-2. Cella

This long rectangular room once housed the altar and a statue dedicated to Quell. The altar was stripped of everything of value and the statue was pulled down and is in fragments on the floor. The interior shows less decay than the outside of the temple, and the reliefs carved in three rows of figures around the upper walls can still be read. The three rows tell the following stories:

The Upper Row

The sea god Quell is resplendent upon a throne of coral as he receives the adulation of all manner of maritime peoples, from simple sailors to grand admirals of the empire. The rest of the reliefs show Quell handing down his beneficence upon the people in the form of good winds, plentiful catches, safe voyages, and terrible storms that wreck invading fleets.

The Middle Row

The reliefs show people disobeying Quell's priests, which results in storms upon the sea. Quell next sounds a conch horn to call forth a mass of tentacles to sink ships and to destroy seaside villages. The tentacles swim beneath Stormwall Temple.

The Bottom Row

The reliefs show a great turtle-like creature with the head of a dragon attacking ships, with people drowning or being consumed in flames. In others, supplicants gather at the base of Quell's coral throne. Quell hands a crown, a scepter, and a toga to a priest standing on the great spire of Stormwall Temple. Finally, the great turtle beast floats listlessly on the waves, as the people rejoice and praise Quell.

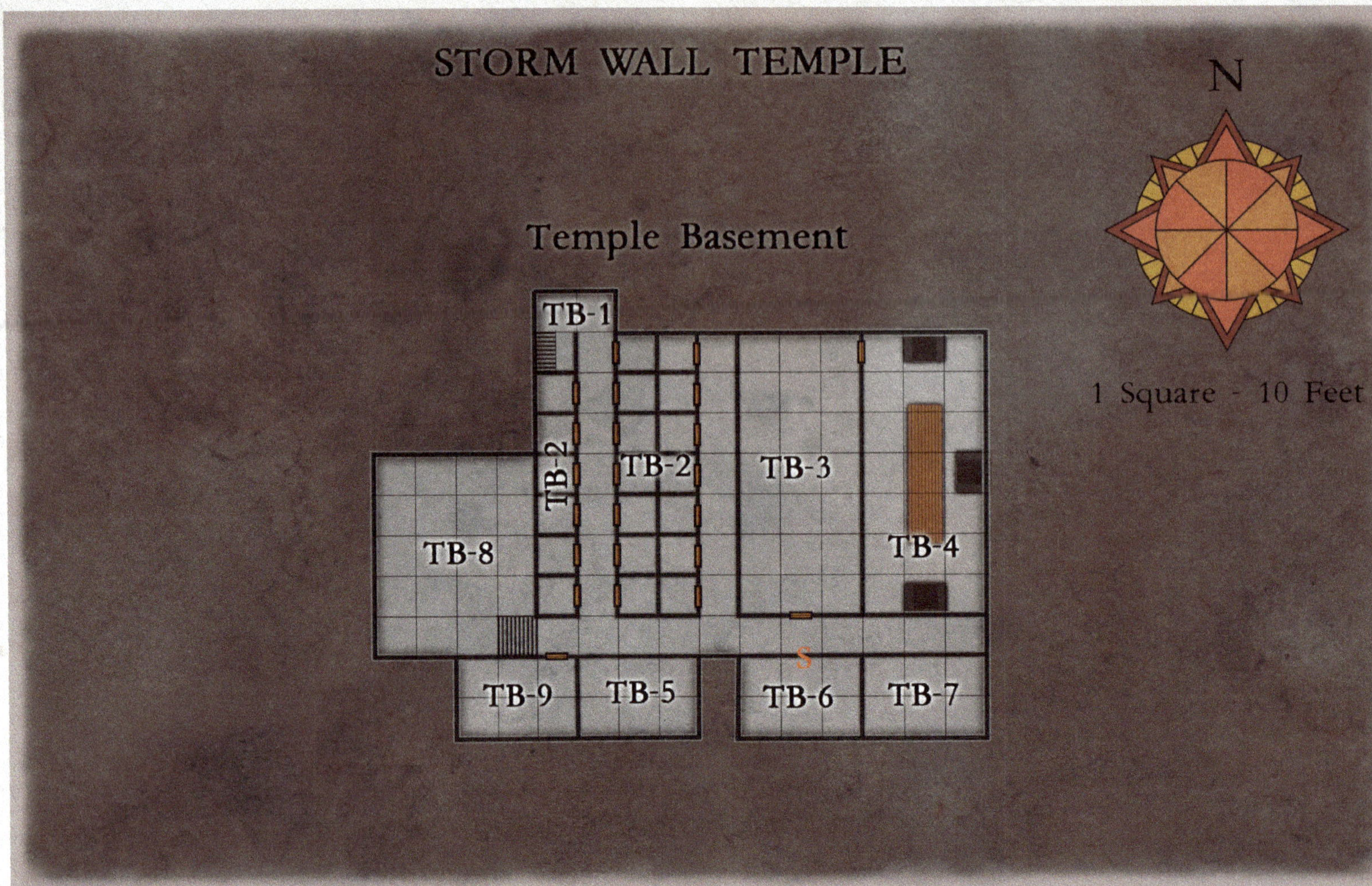

T-3. Opisthodomos

This room in the back of the temple is hidden behind a secret door. The small room behind the door contains a set of stairs that lead down to the temple's basement.

T-4. The Spire Stump

The remains of the great spire stand behind the seaward side of the temple and still connect to the temple proper. Sadly, rubble from the tower fills the hollow base of the stump.

The Temple Basement

The rock of the Hook is a porous limestone not well suited to construction or tunneling, but the brilliant Hyperborean engineers managed to carve out a few small chambers beneath Stormwall Temple. These passages are unlit, of worn but smooth stonework, with 10-foot-wide corridors and eight-foot ceilings. The walls were once covered in frescoes showing various parts of the scriptures of Quell. For the most part, they are faded but intact.

TB-1. Landing

This small room served as a landing for the single flight of stairs up to the temple. The doorways are empty but hinges still hang where they were bolted into the walls.

TB-2. Priests' Quarters

A dozen priests once served Quell in the temple while two dozen more tended small shrines along the Wievin Strip. The quarters here could host the dozen temple priests with plenty of room for another six visitors.

Each room once contained a bed, a dresser, a chest, a table, and a chair. The walls were hung with tapestries depicting scenes from the scriptures of Quell, but these banners are now rotted. Priest-Sergeant Fellblow's troops looted the place and took down any tapestries that might be of value. They tore religious icons from the walls and broke open any locked chests to search for treasure.

TB-3. Dining Hall

In its heyday, priests, acolytes, and others dined and gathered here for non-religious matters. Fellblow's thugs shattered or tossed about the once-orderly rows of benches. The cabinets that held the temple's dining services — finely crafted pieces of silver, turquoise, and coral — were broken open and looted. A few pieces of broken pottery, of fine make and showing religious scenes, are strewn across the flagstone.

TB-4. Kitchens

Three huge fireplaces, their unlit interiors now filled with rubble, stand along one wall. A long sturdy table of aged oak opposite the fireplaces now shows great signs of dry rot. Fellblow was very exacting in his looting and even took the kitchenware, as even centuries-old pots and pans can fetch something at a tinker's cart.

TB-5. High Priest's Quarters

Fellblow's troops thoroughly looted and defaced this once-opulent room, after which a trio of vampire spawn occupied it. The spawn arranged beds of rushes, reeds, and cloth taken from their victims. They keep a small pile of treasure on the only unbroken table they could find in the temple: 50 gp, 89 sp, and 75 cp, and a large ruby valued at 300 gp. During the day, the **3 vampire spawn** reside here, but at night they lurk about the temple or gather in this room to plot and plan. There is a 30% chance on any given night that they are out hunting. One of the vampire spawn wears an exquisite blue toga with coral clasp. This is the *toga of the master of the Island that Dreams* (see **Appendix B: New Magic Items**).

Belsir of Reme, Male Vampire Spawn: HD 5; **HP** 37; **AC** 4[15]; **Atk** bite (1d10); **Move** 12 (fly 18); **Save** 12; **AL** C; **CL/XP** 8/800; **Special:** +1 or better magic weapon to hit, charm gaze (as *charm person*, −1 save), regenerate (1hp/round), shapeshift. (*Monstrosities* 498)
> **Equipment:** *toga of the master of the Island that Dreams* (see **Appendix B: New Magic Items**).

Tala, Female Vampire Spawn: HD 5; **HP** 30; **AC** 4[15]; **Atk** bite (1d10); **Move** 12 (fly 18); **Save** 12; **AL** C; **CL/XP** 8/800; **Special:** +1 or better magic weapon to hit, charm gaze (as *charm person*, −1 save), regenerate (1hp/round), shapeshift. (*Monstrosities* 498)

Tef, Male Vampire Spawn: HD 5; **HP** 33; **AC** 4[15]; **Atk** bite (1d10); **Move** 12 (fly 18); **Save** 12; **AL** C; **CL/XP** 8/800; **Special:** +1 or better magic weapon to hit, charm gaze (as *charm person*, −1 save), regenerate (1hp/round), shapeshift. (*Monstrosities* 498)

TB-6. Shrine of the Kraken

Kaltran did not leave anything behind in this room that could be used against him. He even left the secret panel open so any who came after him could see the damage. The frescoes have been horribly defaced, the ritual implements taken, and the chamber splattered with goat's blood. The frescoes once showed some kind of tentacled creature, but beyond that, the paint is either covered in plaster, gone, or chipped off.

TB-7. Shrine of the Island that Dreams

This small room is open, its secret panel bashed open and in pieces on the floor. A small altar dedicated to Quell is inside, though it has been defaced with a symbol of Mithras carved into its surface. The frescoes remain. They show a great dragon-headed turtle, its attacks on shipping, the high priest of Stormwall Temple calling upon Quell for aid, and the god giving the priest a crown, a scepter, and a toga. The beast is then shown floating in the sea. Instructions on performing the ritual that awakens the Island that Dreams, controls it, and puts it back to sleep are carved into the stone in Hyperborean.

Ritual of the Island that Dreams

If the markings in the hidden shrine are deciphered, they reveal instructions for a lengthy ritual that awakens a creature known as the Island that Dreams. This creature is described as a turtle large enough to carry the world upon its back, or perhaps the weight of the world; the description is archaic and poetic, not to mention rather worn. Once awakened, the Island that Dreams serves the summoner for one lunar phase (seven days) before it returns to its slumber.

The ritual requires a sanctified room (the hidden shrine [**Area TB-7**] is already sanctified for this purpose), ritual components (costing 4,000 gp and available at any city in the Sundered Kingdoms), and three special items: the *crown*, *scepter*, and *toga of the master of the Island that Dreams* (see **Appendix B: New Magic Items**). These three items were stored in the hidden shrine on the pedestals flanking the altar. They are now missing, leaving only vague shapes in the dust.

The ritual itself requires up to five participants. One is designated the leader and makes the required die roll. The ritual takes 14 hours to perform and must be started before the moon rises and completed after it sets. At the end of this time, the leading practitioner must roll below his or her wisdom on 6d6. Each additional participant lowers the result of the roll by 1 (so if five characters participate subtract 4 from the roll for the four participants beyond the one performing the ritual). Each cleric or paladin in the group counts as two for this check (so a party composed of five clerics would subtract 8 from the result, 2 each for the four additional clerics participating in the ritual). If the check fails, the ritual components (but not the special items) are consumed, and the ritual must be attempted again. If the check is failed by 10 or more, the Island that Dreams awakens and goes on a rampage, attacking shipping and settlements along the Wievin Strip until the ritual is repeated to put it back to sleep.

If the ritual is successful, the Island that Dreams awakens and is under the control of the lead practitioner or someone they designate for the duration. The controller can mentally direct the island's actions by thinking commands at it with a range of 20 miles. If not given a command, the island simply floats along, eating whatever passes by. The Island that Dreams is a massive sleeping dragon turtle mistakenly known as for Shell Island. Once the duration of the ritual expires, the island returns to sleep and cannot be summoned for 200 years.

The Island that Dreams, Dragon Turtle: HD 15; **AC** 2[17]; **Atk** 2 claws (1d8), bite (3d10); **Move** 3 (swim 9); **Save** 3; **AL** N; **CL/XP** 17/3500; **Special:** break ships (50% chance to capsize), breathe steam (1/day, 90ft-long cone, damage equal to full creature's hit points). (*Monstrosities* 142)

TB-8. Temple Archives

Down a short flight of steps, a set of bronze doors forced off their hinges sway in the entryway. Beyond lies a room that once housed the temple's archives, but now holds a charred mass of burned papers, books, and scrolls. Sifting through the pile reveals several unburned pages. Most of these are simple accounting pages, tallies of who donated to the temple, and the amounts (which show a pattern of decreasing donations from the Husbridges). A few pieces mention the *Ritual of the Kraken* and the *Ritual of the Island that Dreams*.

TB-9. Temple Treasury

The treasury was forced open, its stone doors cracked into rubble, and the room looted. Careful examination shows a missed secret panel in the baseboard of one wall. Inside this panel are copies of the *Ritual of the Kraken* and the *Ritual of the Island that Dreams*, as well as the *scepter of the master of the Island that Dreams* (see **Appendix B: New Magic Items**).

PART FIVE: TERN ISLAND

Tern Island is a large rocky island in the southern reaches of Kadalon Bay. It is mostly known for its large numbers of seabirds, and the fisherfolk from Ostin have long put in here to gather eggs, feathers, and guano when the fishing is poor. For the most part, they leave the island and its ruined Hyperborean fortress alone, fearing the monsters that have taken up residence there as well as stories of ghosts haunting the ruins.

Kaltran Bel'vir chose the ruined fortress on Tern Island as his base of operations while he works to destroy Ostin. Toward that end, he temporarily relocated his laboratory to the fortress and hired the Sons and Daughters of Strife, a small company of mercenaries, to help protect it.

RANDOM ENCOUNTERS ON TERN ISLAND

Tern Island is rugged and strewn with large rocks, and encounters here occur suddenly and without much warning. Check for encounters for every hour of travel, or every six hours if stationary.

d100	Encounter
01–30	No encounter
31–40	**1–2 ogres** (Bash and Basher from **Area T-3**)
41–50	**2 lightning lizards** (chased out of the ruined fortress)
51–60	Goblin patrol (consists of **2d4 goblins** and a **bugbear**, see Goblin Camp [**Area T-5**])
61–70	**2d10 flying swords**
71–80	**3 doppelgangers** (chased out of the ruined fortress)
81–90	**1d4 + 2 harpies**
91–100	**2d4 skeletons** (Kaltran makes far more undead than he can control and turns the rest loose)

Bash and Basher, Ogres (2): HD 4+1; **HP** 30, 27; **AC** 5[14];
Atk weapon (1d10+1); **Move** 9; **Save** 13; **AL** C; **CL/XP** 4/120;
Special: none. (*Monstrosities* 356)

Bugbear: HD 3+1; **AC** 5[14]; **Atk** bite (2d4) or weapon (1d8+1);
Move 9; **Save** 14; **AL** C; **CL/XP** 4/120; **Special:** surprise
opponents (1–3 on d6). (*Monstrosities* 53)

Doppelganger: HD 4; **AC** 5[14]; **Atk** claw (1d12); **Move** 9; **Save**
13 (5 vs. magic); **CL/XP** 5/240; **Special:** +5 save vs. magic,
immune to sleep and charm, mimic shape. (*Monstrosities* 129)

Flying Sword (Animated Object) (2d10): HD 1; **AC** 6[13];
Atk slash (1d6); **Move** 12 (fly); **Save** 17; **AL** N; **CL/XP** 1/15;
Special: none. (*Monstrosities* 13)

Goblins (2d4): HD 1d6 hp; **AC** 6[13]; **Atk** short sword (1d6);
Move 9; **Save** 18; **AL** C; **CL/XP** B/10; **Special:** –1 to hit in
sunlight. (*Monstrosities* 211)

Harpies (1d4+2): HD 3; **AC** 7[12]; **Atk** 2 talons (1d3) and
weapon (1d6); **Move** 6 (fly 18); **Save** 14; **AL** C; **CL/XP** 4/120;
Special: charm person (touch, as spell, save avoids), siren-song
(drawn toward harpy, save avoids). (*Monstrosities* 240)

Lightning Lizards (2): HD 5; **AC** 3[16]; **Atk** 2 claws (1d4),
bite (1d8); **Move** 12; **Save** 12; **AL** N; **CL/XP** 6/400; **Special:**
immune to electricity, lightning blast (2/day, 4d6 damage, save
for half). (*Monstrosities* 301)

Skeletons (2d4): HD 1; **AC** 8[11] or 7[12] with shield; **Atk**
weapon or strike (1d6) or (1d6+1 two-handed); **Move** 12; **Save**
17; **AL** N; **CL/XP** 1/15; **Special:** immune to sleep and charm
spells. (*Monstrosities* 428)

The following locations are found on Tern Island. For the most part, the island
is rugged and rocky. In many places, the slopes are too steep to climb. Terns and
other seabirds nest here in the tens of thousands, and the entire island is covered in
guano save for around the ruined fortress. Any attempts to move across the island
are revealed by rising flocks of squawking birds.

T-1. Landing

The old Hyperborean landing has largely fallen into the sea, but a 10-foot-long
stump of stone dock remains. The sea flooded over and through the seawall, leaving
the landing exposed to wind and tide. A lone cog, the *Sandy Splash*, is tied up to the
dock and has a small crew of **3 commoners** on board. A freshly worn path leads up
through the overgrown road to the ruined fortress (**Area T-2**).

Commoners, Male or Female Humans (3): HD 4 hp each; **AC** 9[10];
Atk weapon (1d6); **Move** 12; **Save** 18; **AL** L or N; **CL/XP** B/10;
Special: none. (*Monstrosities* 254)

T-2. Ruined Fortress

The ruined fortress is the lair of Kaltran Bel'vir and his minions and is detailed
in **Part Six: The Ruined Fortress**.

T-3. Próxlür's Cave

Among the monsters driven out of the ruined fortress were the **ogre mage
Próxlür** and her mates, the **2 ogres Bash and Basher**. The trio has taken up refuge
in this shallow cave, surviving as best they can hunting birds and foraging for eggs.
This is not the life they had hoped to lead; in better days, Próxlür planned to use
the ruined fortress as her base to build an army and conquer the Wievin Strip. Now
she does little but fume and rage, often taking her anger out on her mates. She is a
cunning foe and readily sides with the characters against Kaltran. Although she is
true to her word, she takes all oaths very literally and readily warps the meaning
and exacting wording to her advantage, such that she can betray her new allies
when the fight with Kaltran is over.

Bash and Basher, Male Ogres (2): HD 4+1; **HP** 30, 27; **AC** 5[14];
Atk weapon (1d10+1); **Move** 9; **Save** 13; **AL** C; **CL/XP** 4/120;
Special: none. (*Monstrosities* 356)

Próxlür, Female Ogre Mage: HD 8; **HP** 50; **AC** 3[16]; **Atk**
longsword (1d12); **Move** 12 (fly 18); **Save** 7 (+1, ring); **AL** C; **CL/
XP** 11/1700; **Special:** regenerate (1hp/round), spell-like abilities.
(*Monstrosities* 359)

Spell-like Abilities: at will—*darkness 15ft radius, invisibility,
polymorph self;* 1/day—*charm person,* cone of frost (60ft range, 20ft
diameter blast, 8d6 damage to all, save for half), *sleep.*

Equipment: longsword, *ring of protection +1,* 2d4 sp.

T-4. Hidden Vale

This Y-shaped flat area is overshadowed by the rocky heights above. Few birds
bother with this darkened valley, making this a guano-free approach across the
island that can be stealthily navigated.

T-5. Goblin Camp

When Kaltran took over the ruined fortress, he drove out all the monsters that
had taken up residence there. A small clan of goblins and bugbears was among
that number. The Bloody Teeth clan now has no home, is unable to leave Tern
Island as they lack boats or the means of building them, and are constantly harried
by Kaltran's servants. The goblins have a small fortified base tucked into a stony
valley on the island's southern end.

Only **30 adult goblins** and **50 young goblins** are in the tribe, as well as **3 bugbears**. They are desperate, hungry, and willing to fight to the death to hold onto what little they still have. However, they are neither suicidal nor are they any less intelligent than others of their kind. While they see the characters as just another group here to make their lives worse, they are willing to parley. **Gutslash**, their leader, is a fearsome warrior, but she is also cunning and wise. If approached peacefully, she listens to proposals and can be talked into helping the characters. At a minimum, she knows the secrets of the fortress, and at most, she can lead her clan in an attempt to remove Kaltran. The latter is predicated on a great deal of trust, as well as the promise that the characters return the fortress to her.

Bugbears (3): HD 3+1; HP 23, 20, 18; AC 5[14]; **Atk** bite (2d4) or longsword (1d8+1); **Move** 9; **Save** 14; **AL** C; **CL/XP** 4/120; **Special:** surprise opponents (1–3 on d6). (*Monstrosities* 53)

Goblins (30): HD 1d6 hp; AC 6[13]; **Atk** short sword (1d6); **Move** 9; **Save** 18; **AL** C; **CL/XP** B/10; **Special:** –1 to hit in sunlight. (*Monstrosities* 211)

Young Goblins (50): HD 1d3 hp; AC 6[13]; **Atk** weapon (1d4); **Move** 9; **Save** 18; **AL** C; **CL/XP** A/5; **Special:** –1 to hit in sunlight. (*Monstrosities* 211)

Gutslash, Female Goblin: HD 6; HP 41; AC 6[13]; **Atk** battle axe (1d8+1); **Move** 9; **Save** 11; **AL** C; **CL/XP** 6/400; **Special:** –1 to hit in sunlight, +1 to hit and damage strength bonus. (*Monstrosities* 211) **Equipment:** battle axe, 2d6 gp.

T-5A. Brush Stockade

The goblins assembled this stockade from driftwood, brush, and stone. It is an impressive barrier, but stands only five feet high.

T-5B. Watchtower

This rickety tower reaches a mere 10 feet into the sky, a climb for a goblin but not terribly impressive for taller races. **Two goblins** are on watch here at any time.

Goblins (2): HD 1d6 hp; HP 5, 3; AC 6[13]; **Atk** short sword (1d6); **Move** 9; **Save** 18; **AL** C; **CL/XP** B/10; **Special:** –1 to hit in sunlight. (*Monstrosities* 211)

T-5C. Chieftain's Hut

Gutslash's hut is slightly larger than the others but not by much. She lives simply so that her tribe might prosper, but there is just not enough to go around. Gutslash is in her hut only during the day; at night, she organizes patrols and does all she can to hold the fractious goblins together.

T-5D. Shaman's Cave

This slit in the rock wall is only eight feet deep and four feet high, just right for a displaced goblin shaman named Bloody Paw. The tribe's spiritual leader is suffering his own spiritual crisis and rarely leaves his cave. He once thought the goblins' deities protected them and provided a fine home in the ruined fortress. But were the sacrifices not appealing? Bloody Paw is so lost in his morose sorrow that he has not prepared spells in some time, and even if the camp is attacked, he does not stir to defend it or himself.

Bloody Paw, Goblin Shaman: HD 4; HP 23; AC 6[13]; **Atk** staff (1d6); **Move** 9; **Save** 13; **AL** C; **CL/XP** 4/120; **Special:** –1 to hit in sunlight, spells (3/2). (*Monstrosities* 211)

Spells: 1st—*charm person, magic missile, sleep*; 2nd—*darkness 15ft radius, web.*

T-5E. Wolf Pen

The goblins managed to save **3 worg wolves** when they fled the ruined fortress. The two male and female wolves are kept here with **6 goblins** guarding them day and night. The wolves are the most well-fed members of the tribe. The goblins hope to rebuild the pack and ride once more to plunder and pillage.

Goblins (6): HD 1d6 hp; HP 6, 5, 4, 3x2, 2; AC 6[13]; **Atk** short sword (1d6); **Move** 9; **Save** 18; **AL** C; **CL/XP** B/10; **Special:** –1 to hit in sunlight. (*Monstrosities* 211)

Worgs (3): HD 4; HP 27, 24, 21; AC 6[13]; **Atk** bite (1d6+1); **Move** 18; **Save** 13; **AL** C; **CL/XP** 4/120; **Special:** none. (*Monstrosities* 515)

T-5F. Spring

A spring of fresh water flows out of the cliff face to form a small pool. Goblins being goblins, this water is fouled with waste, offal, and other debris.

T-6. Old Watchtower

The mercenaries assigned to this stump of a stone watchtower do not like the assignment. There is not much to watch aside from open ocean, the tower is clear across the rocky island, the climb is torturous, and the tower is a ruin. It leaks in the rain, is filled with drafts, and lacks any true comforts. A rain barrel outside provides water, but the **3 guards** on duty must bring their own rations. Needless to say, they do not spend as much time on lookout as they should, and even then tend to gaze off into the distance and daydream whatever thuggish dreams they might have.

Guards, Male or Female Humans (3): HD 3; HP 18 each; AC 7[12]; **Atk** longsword (1d8); **Move** 12; **Save** 14; **AL** C; **CL/XP** 3/60; **Special:** none. (*Monstrosities* 257)

T-7. Secret Cove

A small niche in the rocky shore allows small boats to land, but it is difficult to bring the vessel in without wrecking it on the surrounding cliffs. Kaltran is unaware of this cove, and the guards in the old watchtower (**Area T-6**) can't see it from their vantagepoint.

T-8. Temple Shoals

A small temple to Quell on the island was abandoned and forgotten long before the fortress was built. An earthquake leveled the temple ruins, and the sea flooded over them. These stumps of stonework block the entrance to **Area T-7** during ebb tide, but during high tide a carefully handled boat can slip over the shoal without harm. Large boats and ships founder on the rocks.

PART SIX: THE RUINED FORTRESS

Millennia ago, the Hyperborean Empire built this fortress and secure bay to host a small fleet of ships on anti-piracy duty. As a far-flung bastion of the empire, it was abandoned when the empire started to crumble and has since fallen into ruin. A series of monsters, villains, and would-be pirate lords have occupied it over the years, but none has lasted here for more than a few decades before either being defeated or moving on.

As a native of the Wievin Strip, Kaltran is well aware of the ruined fortress and its history. He chose this as his base of operations for revenge, partly because it suited his purposes and partly because he is amused to cast himself as one of a long series of villains from local myth and legend.

Kaltran Bel'vir can be found anywhere within the ruined fortress but most likely is encountered in the laboratory (**Area LL-2**), the cistern (**Area LL2-2**), or his quarters (**Area LL2-3**). His personal bodyguard **Hrauk** is always found close by.

Kaltran Bel'vir, Male Human Wizard (MU10): HP 36; AC 7[12] or 2[17] (missile) and 4[15] (melee) from *shield* spell; **Atk** *+2 dagger* (1d4+2) or *staff of power* (2d6); **Move** 12; **Save** 4 (+2, ring); **AL** C; **CL/XP** 12/2000; **Special:** +2 vs. spells, wands and staffs, spells (4/4/3/2/2).

Spells: 1st—*charm person, magic missile, read magic, shield*; 2nd—*detect invisibility, ESP, invisibility, phantasmal force*; 3rd—*dispel magic, lightning bolt, hold person*; 4th—*charm monster, dimension door*; 5th—*animate dead, teleport*.

Equipment: *staff of power* (35 charges), *ring of protection +2, potion of extra healing* (x2), *potion of flying*, scroll (*haste, slow*), 2d8 gp.

Hrauk, Hill Giant: HD 8+2; HP 52; AC 4[15]; **Atk** club (2d8); **Move** 12; **Save** 8; **AL** C; **CL/XP** 9/1100; **Special:** throw boulders (2d8 damage). (*Monstrosities* 198)

Hrauk is a hill giant that Kaltran charmed years ago as his first successful experimental subject. Slow-witted even by hill giant standards, Hrauk still obeys Kaltran without question thanks to the sorcerer's work to create a more loyal and trustworthy subject.

FORTRESS DETAILS

Most of the ruined fortress is made from now-crumbling stone. No doors are left unless otherwise noted, and the walls are easy to climb thanks to plenty of handholds in the decaying masonry. The holes in the walls also allow sight through to the other side. The outer walls are 10 feet thick but they have suffered the ravages of time. Several small breaches in the walls are large enough for a small creature to squeeze through, as well as two larger breaches (at **Area P-9**) that have been repaired to some degree, and one large breach that has been overlooked (**Area P-10**).

P-1. NORTHWEST TOWER

This tower crumpled, leaving the upper stories collapsed onto the lower. A pile of rubble blocks the entrance, and none of the mercenaries pays much attention to it.

P-2. NORTHEAST TOWER

The top of this tower fell and collapsed outside the walls, forming a steep slope that leads up to the open top of the now two-story tower. The doors (one facing the north and east walls, as well as one opening onto the courtyard) are newly made and locked from the outside. Kaltran experimented with creating zombies from the mercenaries who died clearing out the fortress, but the rest of the mercenaries complained. Hoping to spare their feelings, Kaltran locked the zombies in this tower. Currently, **8 zombies** are in the tower, although none is currently under Kaltran's control.

Zombies (8): HD 2; HP 8, 7x2, 6x3, 5, 4; AC 8[11]; **Atk** strike (1d8); **Move** 6; **Save** 16; **AL** N; **CL/XP** 2/30; **Special:** immune to sleep and charm. (*Monstrosities* 529)

P-3. SOUTHEAST TOWER

This tower appears to be intact, but its internal support beams are heavily rotted. The mercenaries do not use the tower, and its doorways stand open. Anyone moving around in the tower risks its collapse (3-in-6 chance the tower causes an ominous creak, while a second 1-in-6 check brings the tower down, causing 6d8 points of damage to anyone inside).

P-4. SOUTHWEST TOWER

This tower was shored up and is not at risk of further collapse. It stands a full 40 feet tall, and the mercenaries use it as a watchtower. At least **3 guards** are always on duty here at any time.

Guards, Male or Female Humans (3): HD 3; HP 18 each; AC 7[12]; **Atk** longsword (1d8); **Move** 12; **Save** 14; **AL** C; **CL/XP** 3/60; **Special:** none. (*Monstrosities* 257)

P-5. EAST BARBICAN

This mighty fortification once protected the gates. Now, it is a heap of fallen masonry.

P-6. WEST BARBICAN

The upper levels of this fortification collapsed, but the ground floor's ceiling is holding the weight. It is only a matter of time before it collapses entirely, however.

P-7. KEEP

The keep has completely fallen in on itself, turning the square-walled bastion into a pile of stone and rubble.

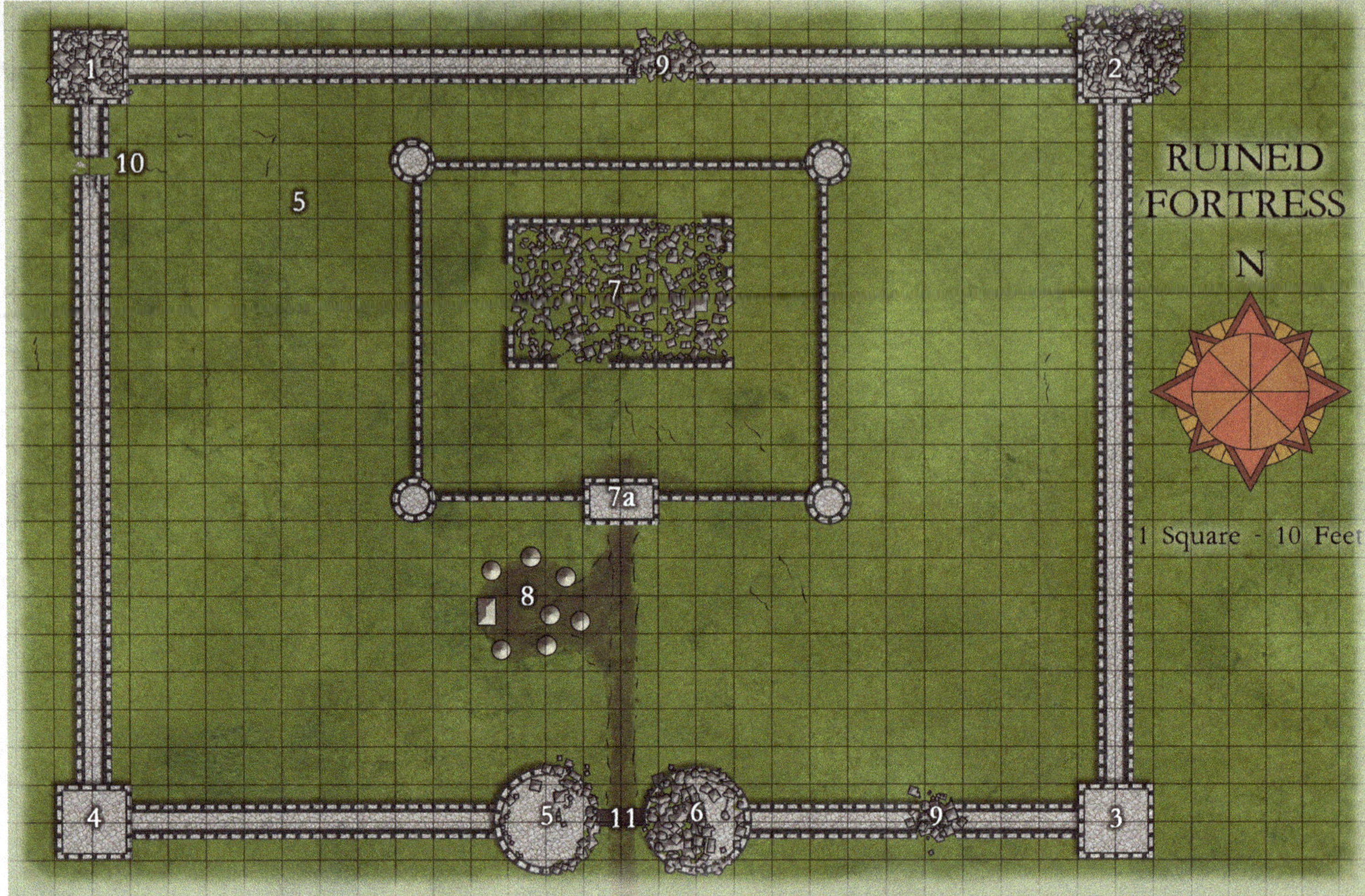

P-7A. Gatehouse

The gatehouse of the keep is still standing and has been shored up. Kaltran found a reference in dusty archives to the fortress on Tern Island having a secret passage into the lower levels. This passage is open and reveals a set of stairs leading down. No doors are on the gatehouse, and the mercenaries do not use it as anything other than a route to the lower levels. If the fight goes against them, they fall back to here and form makeshift barricades at the ground-floor entrances. The ones leading to the fallen walls are already blocked by rubble.

P-8. Mercenary Camp

Kaltran has nearly two dozen remaining mercenaries, the rest having died securing the kraken ritual or clearing out the fortress. **Captain Sergio Teldane** leads the 18 mercenaries (16 are **guards**, while there are **2 berserkers** from the Northlands). They are not loyal to Kaltran but rather to the pay and their sense of honor, in that order. Kaltran is paying them 500 gp a week with a six-month contract. What the mercenaries do not know is that the large payroll Kaltran shows them is actually a mere 10,000 gp with an illusion cast on it to make it look like a larger hoard.

Captain Sergio Teldane, Male Human (Ftr5): HP 33; **AC** 4[15]; **Atk** *+1 longsword* (1d8+1) or light crossbow (1d4+1); **Move** 12; **Save** 10; **AL** C; **CL/XP** 5/240; **Special:** multiple attacks (5) vs. creatures with 1 or fewer HD.

Equipment: chainmail, shield, *+1 longsword*, light crossbow, 20 crossbow bolts.

Berserkers (2): HD 3; **HP** 21, 20; **AC** 7[12]; **Atk** battle axe (1d8); **Move** 12; **Save** 14; **AL** C; **CL/XP** 3/60; **Special:** +2 to hit in berserk state. (*Monstrosities* 255)

Guards, Male or Female Humans (16): HD 3; **HP** 18 each; **AC** 7[12]; **Atk** longsword (1d8); **Move** 12; **Save** 14; **AL** C; **CL/XP** 3/60; **Special:** none. (*Monstrosities* 257)

P-9. Repaired Breach

These large breaks in the wall were repaired by filling them with an eight-foot mound of rubble. The slope is steep but climbable. If they are aware of attackers coming toward a repaired breach, the mercenaries defend them by mounting the mound of rubble and thus gaining higher ground (+1 bonus to hit).

P-10. Overlooked Breach

This narrow breach in the wall was overlooked by Kaltran's mercenaries (you just can't get good help these days). It is only five feet wide at its widest and narrows to three feet at either end, but it is tall enough for medium-sized creatures to pass through.

P-11. Gate

The gate's doors fell and rotted long ago, but the mercenaries constructed a barricade out of a pair of wagons enhanced with wooden panels and spikes. The wagons are drawn by hand in front of the gateway and moved back if needed. There are **2 guards** here day and night.

Guards, Male or Female Humans (2): HD 3; **HP** 18 each; **AC** 7[12]; **Atk** longsword (1d8); **Move** 12; **Save** 14; **AL** C; **CL/XP** 3/60; **Special:** none. (*Monstrosities* 257)

Lower Level 1

The Hyperboreans built several cellars, basements, and other underground features below their fortress, and Kaltran now occupies these. The first level is accessible through the secret passage in **Area P-7A**.

LL-1. Guardroom

A lantern hanging from a hook in the wall lights this small room. **Two guards** are stationed here day and night.
Guards, Male or Female Humans (2): HD 3; **HP** 18 each; **AC** 7[12]; **Atk** longsword (1d8); **Move** 12; **Save** 14; **AL** C; **CL/XP** 3/60; **Special:** none. (*Monstrosities* 257)

LL-2. Laboratory

Kaltran converted this storeroom into his laboratory. The doorway is closed with a curtain; Kaltran has no plans to stay here long term and trusts his mercenaries not to fiddle with things best left alone. The assortment of preserved body parts lining the first bookcase tends to dissuade the curious from poking around. His main interests of exploration and experimentation have been the reshaping of living flesh, though he does dabble from time to time in necromancy. The room holds a large workbench, two bookcases, a cauldron, and a storage box filled with herbs, unguents, and various other items (an enterprising character can root through the box and find 2,000 gp worth of components for either the *Ritual of the Kraken* or the *Ritual of the Island that Dreams*). The workbench is crowded with alchemical and arcane tools, beakers, distillery jars, and similar objects.

Bookcase No. 1

This bookcase is loaded with preserved body parts floating in jars. Pieces of humans, elves, orcs, and other intelligent creatures are found here, as well as parts from a dozen animals and monsters. In between the jars are boxes with useful items such as grave dust, newt eyes, and dried lizard tongues.

Bookcase No. 2

Books, scroll tubes, and rolled maps fill this bookshelf. It contains treatises on Hyperborean history, anatomy, necromancy, the summoning and control of living creatures, the creation of viable undead from mixed parts, and other topics. Kaltran's four volumes of notes are wedged in between the other books. These detail his life story, the history of his adventuring career, and his copy of the *Ritual of the Kraken*, the ceremony he uses to summon and control the kraken. These books would be valuable to the right collector, but several are banned in most civilized nations. All told, the book collection weighs 300 pounds and would fetch 6,000 gp if the right buyers can be found.

LL-3. Antechamber

The bronze doors of this room are some of the few doors still standing in the lower levels. They are sturdy but unlocked and feature iconography of the Mithraic faith. Despite long years of disuse and the fact that no priests are among the mercenaries, many of them are still followers of Mithras and hold ceremonies in this small shrine. The antechamber now sees some use as a gathering place while the rites are prepared or as a place to meditate when off duty. There is a 25% chance that a **guard** is found here in quiet mediation.
Guard, Male or Female Human: HD 3; **HP** 18; **AC** 7[12]; **Atk** longsword (1d8); **Move** 12; **Save** 14; **AL** C; **CL/XP** 3/60; **Special:** none. (*Monstrosities* 257)

LL-4. Vestibule

The faithful of the fortress used this room as their dressing room in preparation for enjoying the mysteries in the rooms farther on. The local celebrants do not carry their full regalia with them, so this room has a small table with crude holy symbols and cowls piled on it.

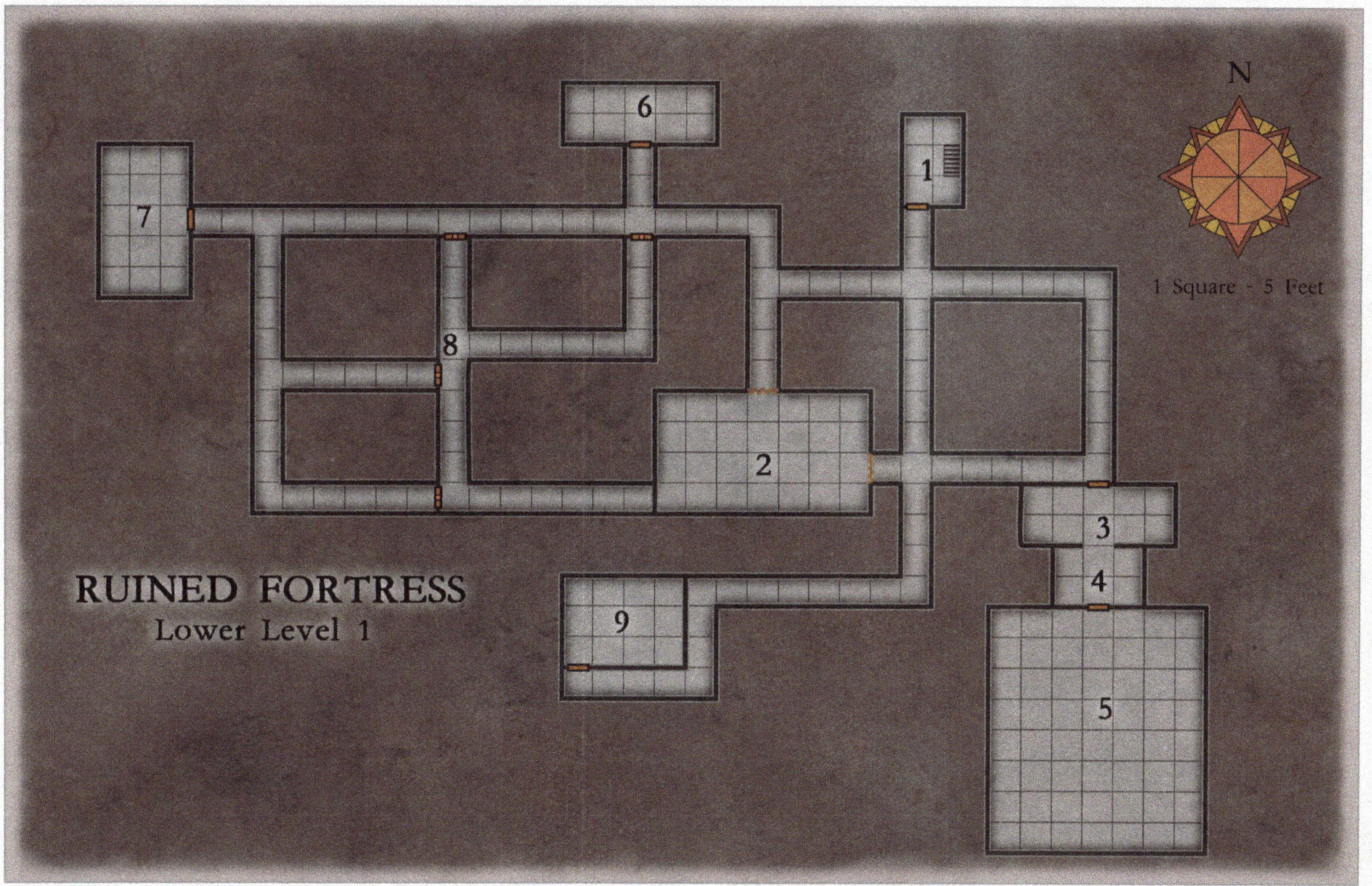

LL-5. Sanctuary

The doors to this room are much like the ones in **Area LL-3**. Beyond lies a disused shrine to the god Mithras. The altar has been redecorated but not officially re-consecrated and holds a small sacrifice of hardtack and salted pork. The walls are painted with frescoes that depict the mysteries of the faith, and a statue of Mithras stands at the far end.

LL-6. Storeroom

This storeroom includes more of Kaltran's belongings, including various mundane items and Kaltran's wardrobe. These fine furs and other clothing are worth 200 gp.

LL-7. Storeroom

Kaltran hasn't fully unpacked and has no plans to do so. This room is protected by a solid, locked wooden door of recent construction. Inside are crates, boxes, and barrels holding Kaltran's samples from various creatures, some of his books, clothing, and other personal effects. If an hour is taken to open all the containers and search through them, 500 gp worth of valuables can be found.

LL-8. Cube Halls

Thick piles of rubble have been carefully stacked and then sealed with crude lime to block off this network of halls. When clearing out the monsters residing in the fortress, Kaltran's mercenaries came across a **gelatinous cube**. Not wanting to risk battle with such a foe, they lured it first one way and then another while hastily constructing the barricades to keep it in. The cube knows there is prey beyond the barricades but lacks the intellect to push on them or otherwise break out. In time, it will starve to death.
Gelatinous Cube: HD 4; HP 26; AC 8[11]; Atk engulf (2d4); **Move** 6; **Save** 13; **AL** N; **CL/XP** 5/240; **Special:** immune to lightning and cold, paralysis (save or paralyzed, 6 turns). (***Monstrosities*** 188)

LL-9. Armory

The mercenaries prefer not to enter the lower levels beneath the fortress, but Kaltran is the boss and he seems to enjoy their discomfort. Thus, he ordered that the armory be placed in this room and that a guard be posted day and night. The armory has a crude door, but it is unlocked. **Two guards** are stationed just outside the door.

Inside are racks of armor (three suits of chainmail, five suits of studded leather), as well as 10 heavy crossbows, 500 bolts, eight halberds, and 16 pikes. In addition, a heavy chest contains the mercenary company's paperwork and ready cash (11,500 gp).
Guards, Male or Female Humans (2): HD 4; HP 26, 21; AC 7[12]; **Atk** longsword (1d8); **Move** 12; **Save** 13; **AL** Any; **CL/XP** 4/120; **Special:** none. (***Monstrosities*** 257)

LOWER LEVEL 2

The lowest level of the fortress's basement is unlit, but a wall sconce every 20 feet holds a torch that is ready to be lit. Being deeper, these hallways are more humid. The walls and floors are slightly slick with condensation, and the temperature is close to 50°, save near the cistern where it drops to 45°.

LL2-1. LANDING

This landing grants access to the second lower level. A small table with three legs leans against the northwest corner and holds flint, steel, and six unlit torches.

LL2-2. CISTERN

This huge basin of fresh water once fed the fortress, but an earthquake centuries ago opened a crack to the sea. Now, the water is too briny to drink. The crack runs for 650 feet to the sea, exiting into the ocean 65 feet below the water. Kaltran likes to call the kraken into the cistern after summoning it, supposedly to personally give it commands. The mercenaries think Kaltran is mad because he likes to talk to the kraken, often spending hours holding one-sided conversations with the mighty beast.

If Kaltran is found here, the kraken (if it is still alive) has a 25% chance of arriving within 2d4+2 rounds.

LL2-3. QUARTERS

Kaltran prefers to work on the level above so that fumes can easily vent out of his laboratory, but he resides in this chamber on the lowest level. Not much is here, as he has never been one given over to luxury. A simple sleeping bag and furs lie in one corner, while a small table holds a standard mess kit and trail rations, and there is a small stack of fine vintages from Bard's Gate (12 bottles, each worth 40 gp). Kaltran is rarely here, as he prefers to spend his time in his laboratory, but he does sleep about six hours every night.

LL2-4. STOREROOM

The lowest level is a bad place to store food, as the damp quickly spoils even salt beef and hardtack. Yet Kaltran insists that the mercenaries use this room as their storehouse. Well, he's the boss, and thus the room is filled with 20 casks of ale, 50 crates of hardtack, 16 hanging flanks of salted meat, and three casks of wine. The mercenaries normally place guards on any alcohol they have, but given the conditions they are serving under, their captain decided to forget about that.

ENDING THE ADVENTURE

Assuming the characters stop Kaltran or at least his kraken, they are hailed as heroes in Ostin. The mayor asks them to remain until after the grulin run, but understands if they want to go off on new adventures. Their pay amounts to 5,000 gp each, but after a successful grulin run, the town can offer an additional 8,000 gp bonus. However, that won't be for another six to eight weeks. There are plenty of places to adventure until then, as the Wievin Strip contains many secrets and threats.

There is also the issue of Baroness Husbridge. If she is killed hunting the kraken, she dies without an heir. This leaves her small keep and title up for grabs, and this can provide a base for conquering heroes. With the townsfolk of Ostin as their supporters and the peoples of the Wievin Strip ready for good leadership, the successful conclusion of this adventure should set the characters up well for the move to titled landowner and their transition from wandering adventurers to petty rulers.

Finally, there is Kaltran. Defeating the kraken does not defeat him, and if he escapes, he returns later. Naturally, he will be more powerful and will bring with him a new means to fulfill his vengeance upon Ostin. What manner that may take is up to you, but keep in mind that he is intelligent, driven, and completely amoral.

Bog Hag

Hit Dice: 7
Armor Class: 2[17]
Attacks: 2 claws (2d4 + poison)
Saving Throw: 9
Special: +1 or better magic weapons to hit, create bog zombie, darkvision, immune to poison, magic resistance, poison, resist cold and fire, spell-like abilities
Move: 12/12 (swimming)
Alignment: Chaos
Number Encountered: 1
Challenge Level: 11/1700

This rare type of hag lives in peat bogs, foul swamps, and other areas so fetid and decayed that even other hags wrinkle their already wrinkly noses at it. Bog hags are much like other hags, deadly fey who prefer to feed on the flesh of mortals, it is just that they prefer that flesh to steep a bit in a nice ripe bog. Often they seek to take over local villages to ensure a steady supply of victims as well as to provide them with the worship and tribute they so desperately feel is owed them.

Bog hags are tied to a particular bog from which they draw their power and where they steep their kills. Any creature slain in the bog ruled by the hag rises in seven days as a bog zombie. Their vicious claws are coated in the foulness of the swamp, and any creature struck by the hag must make a saving throw or suffer as its flesh begins to rot.

Bog Hag: HD 7; AC 2[17]; Atk 2 claws (2d4 + poison); **Move** 12 (swim 12); Save 9; AL C; CL/XP 11/1700; **Special:** +1 or better magic weapons to hit, create bog zombie (slain victims rise within 7 days), darkvision (60ft), immune to poison, magic resistance (10%), poison (save or flesh rots, 1d6 damage per day until healed), resist cold and fire (50% damage), spell-like abilities.

Spell-like abilities: at will—*darkness 15ft radius, phantasmal force*; 2/day—*magic missile, polymorph self, suggestion*.

Bog Zombie

Hit Dice: 3
Armor Class: 7[12]
Attacks: strike (1d8)
Saving Throw: 14
Special: immune to sleep and charm, stench, vulnerable to fire
Move: 12/12 (swimming)
Alignment: Neutrality
Number Encountered: 1d4, 2d6
Challenge Level: 3/60

The bodies of a bog hag's victims are often steeped in the fetid ground of her home bog to ripen to her foul tastes. Sometimes, however, the bog hag allows the deceased to rise after seven days as a bog zombie that faithfully serves its fey mistress. These peat-covered creatures are slightly tougher zombies, but are vulnerable to flames because of the decaying swamp plants wrapping their bodies. Anyone within 10 feet of a bog zombies must make a saving throw or suffer a −1 penalty to hit and damage due to the incredible stench.

Bog Zombie: HD 3; AC 7[12]; Atk strike (1d8); **Move** 6 (swim 9); Save 14; AL N; CL/XP 3/60; **Special:** immune to sleep and charm, stench (10ft radius, save or −1 to hit and damage), vulnerable to fire (200% damage).

APPENDIX B: NEW MAGIC ITEMS

GREATER MISCELLANEOUS MAGICAL ITEMS

CROWN OF THE MASTER OF THE ISLAND THAT DREAMS

The wearer of this silver crown set with ocean-blue sapphires can cast the following spells: at will—*purify water*; 3/day—*create water*; 2/day—*water breathing*; 1/week—*part water*. Usable by all classes.

SCEPTER OF THE MASTER OF THE ISLAND THAT DREAMS

This oak scepter is ringed by silver wave-like bands that rise to the tip, which is topped by an aquamarine gem. The *+2 scepter* deals 1d6 points of damage with a successful strike, or 2d6 points of damage to water-based creatures. Usable by all classes.

TOGA OF THE MASTER OF THE ISLAND THAT DREAMS

This blue toga with a coral clasp functions as a *cloak of protection +1* and also allows the wearer to swim at a rate of 12. Usable by all classes.

COMBINING THE CROWN, SCEPTER, AND TOGA

If a single wearer wields the crown, scepter and toga, that character gains all of the benefits of the individual items, but also can walk on water at their normal movement rate. At will, the wielder can also *speak with animals* (aquatic and amphibious creatures only). Once per month, the wielder can summon a water elemental to serve for one week.

Water Elemental: HD 12; AC 2[17]; **Atk** strike (3d10); **Move** 6 (swim 18); **Save** 3; **AL** N; **CL/XP** 13/2300; **Special:** +1 or better magic weapons to hit, overturn boats (sink vessel in 1d4+4 rounds). (***Monstrosities*** 157)

The items can also be combined to complete the ritual to awaken the Island that Dreams as detailed in the adventure.

NECROMANCER
Games™